BATTLE OF THE BRIDGE

Almost before he knew it, the High Lord Demetrios was in among the enemy cavalry, his huge stallion easily bowling over their smaller, lighter mounts. Then, suddenly, an ax split his stallion's skull, and Demetrios found himself afoot in the midst of a cavalry engagement. Caught in a deadly dangerous position, and with his badly depleted Confederation troops being forced step by step back across the bridge, there was only one thing for him to do. As a lancer thundered down upon him, Demetrios avoided the lance point, grasped the shaft, and jerked. Then, while the foeman was still unbalanced, he grabbed the right foot and heaved, then clawed his way up into the empty saddle, and spurred his new mount forward in a frantic attempt to rejoin his own army. . . .

SWORDS
OF THE
HORSECLANS

A Horseclans Novel

by

Robert Adams

A SIGNET BOOK

NEW AMERICAN LIBRARY

PUBLISHER'S NOTE

This book is a work of fiction. Names, characters, places, and incidents are either the product of the author's imagination or are used fictitiously, and any resemblance to actual persons, living or dead, events or locales is entirely coincidental.

NAL BOOKS ARE AVAILABLE AT QUANTITY DISCOUNTS WHEN USED TO PROMOTE PRODUCTS OR SERVICES. FOR INFORMATION PLEASE WRITE TO PREMIUM MARKETING DIVISION, NEW AMERICAN LIBRARY, 1633 BROADWAY, NEW YORK, NEW YORK 10019.

Published by arrangement with the author

SIGNET TRADEMARK REG. U.S. PAT. OFF. AND FOREIGN COUNTRIES REGISTERED TRADEMARK—MARCA REGISTRADA HECHO EN CHICAGO, U.S.A.

SIGNET, SIGNET CLASSIC, MENTOR, ONYX, PLUME, MERIDIAN AND NAL BOOKS *are published by NAL PENGUIN INC., 1633 Broadway, New York, New York 10019*

FIRST SIGNET PRINTING, AUGUST, 1981

9   10   11   12   13   14   15   16   17

This book is dedicated to my mother,
To my sister, Loula,
To my nephew, Danny, and
To my nieces, Cherie and Tess;
To my good and most talented friends,
Gordy Dickson and André Norton,
To Gail and Alan Kaufman and
To Jack and Cherry Weiner

Author's Preface

When called upon, at cons and elsewhere, to categorize the books making up my HORSECLANS SERIES, I label them "Heroic Adventure Fantasies" rather than the more familiar "Science Fiction," "Science Fantasy" or something similar. I am not a scientist and you will find damn-all science in my writings.

Nor will you find much moralization, since I strongly feel that too many of today's fictional offerings are less books, to be read and enjoyed, than they are soapboxes, from which their authors feel free to preach and preach and preach, *ad nauseum*.

HORSECLANS books are escapist literature, pure and simple. They are conceived and written expressly for the enjoyment of you, the reader, for your pleasure and relaxation, not to make points for my own particular politico-sociologico-economico-ethnico-religious views.

Enjoy!

Robert Adams

Richmond, Virginia

SWORDS
OF THE
HORSECLANS

1

Briskly, the column of horsemen trotted onto the long, ancient bridge, steel-shod hooves ringing on the worn stones. Behind them, an oncoming dustcloud heralded the advance of their army; before them, across the width of the river, the empty road wound into the dark density of a forest, beyond which rose the mountains that sheltered their foe, King Zenos of Karaleenos.

Leading the column, astride a tall black stallion of the Middle Kingdoms' breed, was a flashily attired man of uncertain age but of obvious Ehleenoee antecedents. His three-quarter armor was plated with gold, silver, and burnished copper, and his lobsterback helmet bore a nodding crest of bright red plumes. The small buckler on his left arm was also gold-plated and bore the Three Rivers sign of his house executed in turquoise. Over his left hip jutted the hilt of his sword—solid gold, pommel and quillons set with rubies, emeralds, and sapphires.

Some few of the men who followed were garbed in a similar manner, but most were not. Only the courtier-officers aped the impractical equipage of Demetrios, Undying High Lord of Kehnooryos Ehlahs. For the real soldiers, who constituted the bulk of the column, it was Pitzburk-plate iron-rimmed bullhide bucklers and steel-and-leather sword hilts wound with brass wire to give a better grip.

The courtiers rode on; silently, behind their perpetually smiling faces, they cursed the dust and the heat, the sweat and discomfort and thirst. But the true soldiers were troubled

1

by other matters. They squirmed uneasily in their sweat-slicked saddles and exchanged worried glances. Those who might have communicated with their fellows by mindspeak kept their mindshields rigidly in place, for Demetrios, too, possessed mindspeak; further, he owned the power of life and death over every officer and man in the army and his temper was notoriously as vicious as his moods were capricious.

Captain Herbuht Mai, commander of a thousand lancers contracted to the service of Kehnooryos Ehlahs, dropped his reins onto his big gelding's neck and commenced to tighten the points securing his helmet.

He hasn't changed, he thought. *He's the same arrogant, overconfident ass that he was forty years ago when grandpa served him! By my steel, he has campaigned with Lord Milo, he should know better. Irregulars should, this very minute, be harrying, nibbling at young Zenos' army, reporting back to us of its strength . . . and its weaknesses. But that pompous popinjay up there doesn't even send out flank riders or point riders, and here we are marching through hostile country.*

Guhsz Helluh, a stocky, fortyish, graying man, had lifted his heavy target from its carrying hooks and was tightening the armstraps, even while his blue-green eyes attempted to peel back the tangle of forest ahead, that he might see what lay under those trees. Though his thin lips fluttered, his words were as silent as had been Mai's, for if the High Lord took it into his head to have him executed, all of his twelve hundred Kweebai pikemen would not be enough to save him.

Damn fool, he thought. *Good fighter—oh, that I admit, in personal combat. But as a strategist or tactician, he can't find his hairy arse with both hands! Three—count 'em—no less than three ambuscades in the last week, and that Undying imbecile still keeps sacrificing security for speed, hurrying good lads to their death for no good reason. He may be immune to steel, but by the Sacred Sword, the rest of us aren't! And that copulating forest could hide anything—a thousand archers or five hundred lancers, even a battery or two of catapults or spearthrowers, and we'd never see them until they were ready.*

But both men were wrong in their estimates of the High Lord. Demetrios rode fully aware of the chances he was taking . . . and he was completely cognizant of the terrible cost should his judgment prove faulty.

Ever since that day, nearly two-score years ago, when he had fought his first single combat with old Alexandros, goaded the aged strahteegos into giving him the death thrust that unexpectedly proved him to be immortal, then joined forces with Lord Milo and his tribe of barbarians, had he been afforded the treatment of a retarded child. True, he admitted to acting the fool in the first flush of his realization that there were but three others like himself in all Kehnooryos Ehlahs. No sooner had he granted equal status to Lord Milo, proclaimed him co-High Lord, than his—Demetrios'—power began to flow away like water runs through a sieve. Then, Milo and his bitch of a wife chivvied him into marrying that renegade slut, Aldora. Even had he liked women, which he did not, Aldora would have been difficult for him to stomach—born an Ehleeneeas, yet she had become more of a barbarian than any other member in the tribe since her adoption into one of the clans.

I tried, he thought, squinting his eyes against the glare that the morning sun threw from his brilliant armor and shield. Gods, but I tried. Nothing is wrong with me, I have no trouble at all with a clean, beautiful boy, but sex with a filthy, incessantly yapping woman is something that a man of my refined sensibilities just cannot perform. And in thirty-odd years that slimy whore has put more horns on my head than a hundred flocks of goats could sport! She flaunts *her* lovers before me and, when I slew one of them, what did she do but seduce *my* favorite lover, ruined the poor boy for life, she did. He'd fathered three or four children on some clanswoman before he died at the intaking of Eeleeoheepolis . . . and it served the faithless pig right—he should have been tortured to death.

And when *my* armies took the field against the northern barbarians and the western barbarians, and during the years it took to win back the north half of Karaleenos, they made a mere puppet of me. Oh, yes, a figurehead, that's all I was! Parading the army before me, calling me captain of commanders, while *they* gave every meaningful order.

As his mount crossed the midpoint of the bridge, Demetrios smiled and, straightening in the saddle, struck a heroic pose, head high and right fist on armored right thigh. Well, I bided my time, I did; now, I've done it. Now I'm in southern Karaleenos, and *I* will wrest it from Zenos, or every man in this army will die in the attempt! Then they'll all know that Demetrios is a man to be reckoned with. They'll . . .

But there was no more time for quiet thought. A sleet of arrows fell upon the head of the column and Demetrios was hard put to control his screaming, wounded horse. None of the men were injured, for the bone-tipped hunting shafts shattered on armor and would not even pierce leather. But the horses were not so well protected; two were down, hampering the column, and several more were hurt.

Captain Helluh spotted the first stone coming and instinctively raised his shield, but the foot-thick boulder was short, splashing into the river yards from the bridge downstream. The second raised a brown geyser about the same distance upstream.

"Bracketed," groaned Herbuht Mai. "The next stone will draw blood unless that ninny has the brains to retreat."

The third stone took out a yard of bridge railing and some of the flying splinters peppered Demetrios' stallion, at which the tortured horse surged forward, bit in teeth, nearly unseating his rider. Despite many misgivings, the column followed as best they could.

While his companions drew swords or readied lances or uncased darts, Mai unslung his horn and winded the signal upon which he and his lieutenants had agreed. Once, twice, thrice he blew the code, then slung the horn and drew his steel.

Seeing where he was being borne, Demetrios drew his sword—no mean feat at a full, jarring gallop—and waved it first over his head, then pointed it at the forest, meanwhile hoping that his horse would stop before he reached the border of the Witch Kingdom, three hundred miles to the south. But he need not have worried; the commander of the ambush knew well the vulnerability of dismounted archers and catapult men to cavalry attack. Within the forest, drums rolled and, before the runaway had reached the southern end of the bridge, a mixed lot of lancers and irregular cavalry debouched from hidden trails onto the roadway. No sooner were half a hundred of the enemy on the road than they launched a counter-charge.

Captain Helluh smiled grimly. Those posturing courtiers would take the brunt of the attack. It would be most interesting to see how well the amateurs received it.

They received it well enough. Any species will fight if cornered; besides, they feared Demetrios more than the enemy horsemen.

Almost before he knew it, Demetrios was in among Zenos' cavalry. His pain-maddened stallion completely bowled over the smaller, lighter mount of an irregular axman. Then the well-trained war horse went to work with teeth and hooves, savaging horseflesh or manflesh impartially. Demetrios turned a lance with his shield and throat-thrust its wielder. A dart clanged off his breast-plate, then an unarmored mountain irregular—wild-eyed and bearded—was raining blow after blow with a woodsman's ax. Demetrios was able to deflect each blow with his battered shield, but found himself unable to use his sword until the stallion sunk big, yellow teeth into his opponent's unprotected thigh. The ax split the stallion's skull, but half the length of the sword had already penetrated the axman's abdomen.

Demetrios was afoot in the midst of a cavalry engagement. There was but one thing to do. Savagely, he sawed loose the armstraps with his bloody sword and dropped the bent and useless shield. A lancer thundered down upon him. Demetrios avoided the point, grasped the shaft, and jerked. Then, while the foeman was still unbalanced, he grabbed the right foot and heaved, then clawed his way up into the empty saddle.

Once on his new horse, the High Lord found he was headed the right way. What was left of his fifty men now outnumbered ten to one, was slowly withdrawing. Only a single blow fell upon him as he spurred his horse forward. He supposed most of Zenos' troopers thought him one of their own.

Herbuht Mai was now in the forefront of the brisk little fight, and all the courtiers were dead, having followed their lord into the enemy's ranks. The powerful captain used his shieldboss to smash a face to red ruin, while his heavy sword sheared off the arm of a lancer. A buffet on his helm set his head to swimming and he almost struck the High Lord before he recognized him.

Inch by hard-fought inch, the little band, now less than half their original number, was forced back across the bridge. Not a horse but was wounded and hardly a man; armor and shields were hacked and shattered, swords nicked and dulled. No darts and few lances remained in use; only sword and dirk were fitted to this kind of combat. Footing for Zenos' troops was treacherous; the bridgebed was blood-slimy and cobbled with dropped weapons and the trampled corpses of men and horses. The forest archers tried one volley, but so many of their own horsemen suffered for it that another was out of the question.

Demetrios longed for his big, black stallion. The lancer's roan gelding was not war-trained. He spent as much time fighting to keep the horse in line as he did hacking at the on-coming forces, and only the excellence of his armor had kept biting steel out of his body. He vowed that, if the roan sur-vived the battle, he would have the cursed beast roasted alive! An irregular came at him with a long-bladed hunting spear, but his small mount stumbled on a still-wriggling body and he struggled to retain his seat. Demetrios stood in his stirrups and, swinging his wide sword with both hands, decapitated the spearman. So great was the press that the corpse could not fall from his saddle. He remained erect, arms jerking spasmodically, twin streams of blood gushing from what re-mained of his thick neck.

A war horse snapped at the roan and, panicked, he backed away through the stone-smashed gap in the railing. The horse struggled to regain the bridge and might have made it, had not a stray sword stroke gashed his tender nose. It was thirty feet to the river. Horse and rider struck the water together in a mighty splash. Both weighted with armor and equipment, they quickly sank beneath.

2

————•••—◆—•••————

"I saw him go over into the river, my lord," said Captain Mai. "But, at that time, it was all I could do to stay alive. We were eighteen or twenty against three or four hundred; indeed, there are but twelve of us breathing tonight."

The tall, saturnine man across the camp table raised a hand and reassured him, saying, "No one is blaming you, Herbuht, least of all, me. Demetrios is a fool. I can't imagine what variety of feather got up his arse to try to mount this kind of campaign with an imbalanced and ill-supplied force of the type he assembled. It's to your everlasting credit that you and Guhsz were able to take what you had at hand and trounce Zenos as badly as you did; you'll, none of you, be forgotten—my word on it."

"And mine as well." The voice came from the tent's entrance. "I just hope the perverted swine is dead. Do you think he could be, Milo?"

Mai arose so rapidly that he overturned his stool, his dark-haired guest simply turned in his chair.

"Hello, Aldora. What kept you?"

The striking woman who entered was as dark as Milo. When she removed her helm and tossed it on Mai's camp bed, it could be seen that her long, coal-black hair had been braided and then, Horseclans-fashion, coiled about her small head to provide padding. The features of her weather-browned face were fine and regular. Her black eyes flashed in the lamplight. Despite her heavy, thigh-high boots, she moved

7

gracefully to the table and took both of Mai's calloused hands in her own. "How long has it been, sweet Herbuht?"

Captain Mai flushed deeply, looking at his toes. "Ten . . . no, eleven years, my lady."

Milo Morai had seen her play this game with other former lovers. Impatiently, he snapped, "For all you know, Aldora, your husband is lying on the bed of the Luhmbuh River, providing a feast for happy fish. You may hate him, but he *is* my co-regent and the only one with a hereditary claim to the rulership of Kehnooryos Ehlahs. Besides, he is one of *our* kind."

Aldora snorted. "And I hope the fish get more use from Demetrios than ever I did! *You* know how it's been between us for the thirty-two years we've been married. Emotionally speaking, Demetrios is—*was*, I pray, Wind—a child, a terribly spoiled brat. Damn it, he looks so masculine, but even if he lives as long as you have, he'll never mature into a real man. He can take all the grandiose titles he can think of, deck himself out in the fanciest clothing and armor he can find, and he'll never be more than a gilded cowpat. He . . ."

"Aldora," Milo said, "we are not alone."

She shook her head defiantly. "We do not need to be. Herbuht was my lover for four years; he's heard all I've said here and more—much, much more. My husband, the Lord High Buggerer of Kehnooryos Ehlahs, is as useful to a woman as is a gelding to a mare! I pray to the Sun and Wind that he be dead. *Oh, Wind grant that I am at last freed of him.*"

Suddenly, she raised both arms, threw back her head and, with closed eyes, began to chant, "Wind, oh, Wind of all Wind. Wind of the North, Wind of the West, Wind of the South, Wind of the East. Oh, Wind of the oceans, Wind of the mountains, Wind of the plains. Wind of gentleness, Wind of violence. Oh, Wind, hear now thy true daughter, Aldora of Linsee, come to me and grant my prayer. Come to me, oh, Wind. Speak to thy daughter, thy servant, thy bride. Come, oh, Wind. Come, come, come, come, *come!*"

From the camp about them came shouts of alarm along with much noise from the picket lines—the snortings and whinnyings of terrified horses. Then a roaring commenced, growing louder as it neared. Then it was all around the tent, and suddenly the front flaps billowed inward, while the heavy lamps hung from the ridgepole were swung to and fro like ships tossed on a stormy sea.

Icy air buffeted Milo's skin and he could not repress a shudder. Aldora's talents continued to amaze him. Speaking in as calm a voice as he could muster, he admonished, "That's more than sufficient, Aldora. The men outside may have to fight tomorrow; they need their relaxation, their dinners, their sleep, and so do the horses."

After a somewhat shaky Herbuht Mai had left to see to his men and to the other captains who had met with King Zenos subsequent to the battle that followed the bridge skirmish, Milo had other words for Aldora.

As he unstrapped her cuirass, he spoke sternly. "You call Demetrios a child, then follow with a completely childish example of mental trickery! Who were you trying to impress, girl? Me? Herbuht Mai?"

She turned to face him, her face looking drained, the halves of her cuirass dangling loose. "It was no trick, Milo. Calling the Wind was one of the secret things Blind Hari taught me before he left."

"If you've known it that long," demanded Milo, "why is it I've never seen you do it before?"

The woman extended trembling arms so that Milo might pull off the armor. "Because I don't do it often, Milo, because it tires me, it takes too much from me."

Drawing off her armor, Milo said angrily, "Don't ever do that at sea, Aldora. There are not very many ways to kill our kind, but drowning *is* one of them."

The four captains—Herbuht Mai of the lancers, Guhsz Helluh of the heavy infantry, Prestuhn Maklaud of the horse-archers, and Gabros Zarameenos of the light infantry—entered and saluted first Milo, then Aldora.

"Lord Milo," spoke Mai, "I have ordered Lord Demetrios' pavilion pitched on that low hill between the camp and the river. It's an exposed position, true, but it will be well guarded. Besides, King Zenos struck me as a man of his word. I don't think he'd allow an attack without formally notifying us of the cessation of the truce."

"That was very thoughtful, Captain." Milo smiled. "I'd

frankly given my quarters no thought, and the only baggage
we brought was two packmules, the bulk of our effects being
with the main army. What think you, gentlemen? Will we be
needing the army? Will Zenos fight again?"

Guhsz Helluh said slowly, "He's a brave man, Lord Milo,
a determined man, and I doubt me not were it up only to
him he'd resist to the last drop of his blood. But fully sixty
percent of his ragtag army was killed or wounded the day before yesterday. I think he'll husband what he has left to build
a new army around."

"Now I'll pose another question, gentlemen." Milo leaned
back in his chair, steepling his fingers. "Captain Mai has
sketched the rough outline of your three ambushes, the skirmish at the bridge, and the full-scale battle beyond it. For all
five actions, what were your losses? Captain Helluh, how
many killed and wounded in your pikemen's ranks?"

Helluh hissed through his gapped teeth. "Too many, my
lord. There'll be many a red eye in Kweebai, and no mistake.
One hundred sixteen were slain, two hundred and thirty
wounded. That's as of sundown tonight, of course. More of
the wounded will certainly die."

"Captain Zarameenos?"

The dark-haired Ehleenoee rumbled from his massive
chest, "I mean not to make excuses, Lord Milo, but the army
was just too tired to fight well, men and horses alike."

Milo nodded. "There will be no recriminations, gentlemen.
All conditions considered, you and your men performed a
near miracle. But, back to your casualties, Captain
Zarameenos."

The big officer nodded briskly, his black spikebeard bob-
bing. "I marched out of Kehnooryos Ehlahs with four thousand men; as of sundown tonight I had three thousand
twenty-two effectives, six hundred forty-nine wounded, and
three hundred twenty-nine are dead."

Mai had lost about a fifth of his squadron, he reported.
Maklaud, whose reddish hair, wiry body, and vulpine face
had combined to give him his nickname of "Foxy," gave the
Horseclans salute and said, "God-Milo, give us Horseclansmen steel armor and these big horses and we're damned hard

to kill! I lost ninety men from six clans, all gone to Wind, no wounded who can't ride and fight."

Milo grinned. "Who'll collect the bounty on your ear, Foxy?"

The other three captains roared and Aldora managed a tired smile. Maklaud reached up to touch the bandages covering what was left of his left ear. "I didn't even know it was gone until after the big fight. It must have happened at the bridge. My helmet took a blow meant for Old Thunder, here," he said, digging a sharp elbow into Zarameenos' ribs, "and the bastard's sword stuck. I couldn't see the Maklaud of Maklaud riding around Karaleenos wearing a sword on his head, so I backed out of line long enough to doff them both—helm and sword. But I'd gotten another helm off one of Zenos' expired officers before the big fight."

Milo leaned forward. "Wait a minute! All four of you were in on the skirmish at the bridge."

He was answered by four nods.

Milo slammed one big fist against his thigh. "Well that ass! He could have lost every senior officer in his so-called command. Thirty-six years of campaigning haven't taught my esteemed co-regent a thing!"

Aldora sighed resignedly. "*I* could have told you that, Milo. Demetrios never learns anything he doesn't *want* to learn. Sun knows, I hope he's dead!"

Milo, Aldora, and their bodyguards sat with the four captains on the mossy northern bank of the Luhmbuh River. A few paces to their rear the tethered horses contentedly cropped grass, all shaded by the huge, ancient trees. In the river, several large rafts had been lashed to the bridge supports and, from them, divers were scouring the muddy bottom of the river. No one was sure exactly where Demetrios had left the bridge, since a good portion of the railing had been torn loose later in the fight and a good many horses and riders had plunged into the river. Therefore, the divers worked from the center toward the south bank.

While the captains chatted and the bodyguards diced and Aldora stared broodingly at the waters of the river, Milo pondered. Should he send word to the main army to march, despite the danger from the west? If that shaky alliance of mountain tribes should attack while most of the army was fourteen days' march away . . . hmmm, it would be bad. On the other hand, should young Zenos be allowed to form another army and cement his present bonds with the Southern Kingdom . . . maybe even ally himself with the Sea Lord and his pirates? It might be best to scotch this Zenos while we've the opportunity. And it shouldn't be all that difficult—not now, not after the drubbing he took the other day.

His eyes closed as he mused, Milo was unaware of the approach of Halfbreed until the cat's chin was resting on his armored thigh. He scratched the furry ears, eliciting a deep sigh of contentment.

Though a great-grandson of mighty Horsekiller, the cat-chief who had led his clan to this land, he had been gotten on a tree cat that had been caught as a kitten and tamed by Aldora; therefore, he was less than two-thirds the bulk of an adult prairie cat. Some seven feet overall, Halfbreed was slender and wiry, his cuspids were only slightly longer than had been his mother's—nowhere near the size of a prairie cat's massive fangs—and his fur was short and uniformly pale brown. Because of his distinct resemblance to his wild cousins, Halfbreed was a very useful scout.

Scanning Milo's surface thoughts, the cat mindspoke a question. "If you mean to fight, God-Milo, should not Halfbreed take a look at the Ehleenee army?"

Milo sighed. "I wish you could, cat-brother. But this river is a natural line of defense. It is wide and deep and there are no fords for many miles. This bridge is the only way across and you could never traverse it unseen . . . not in daylight, anyway—perhaps tonight, if there is no moon or a storm. But wait for my word."

One of Captain Mai's officers came galloping the length of the bridge, ironshod hooves striking sparks. Before his mount had fully halted, the rider was out of his saddle and saluting his captain.

"Sir, a herald from the camp of King Zenos is at the middle of the bridge. He begs audience with High Lord Milo and High Lady Aldora. He is alone and bears only sword and dirk. Besides, I don't think he'd be very dangerous; he's wounded."

When, at length, the officer returned, he rode stirrup to stirrup with a freckle-faced young man in the uniform of Zenos' bodyguards. The wicked tip had been removed from his lance and a square of lustrous, creamy silk fluttered at the apex of the long ash shaft. Nothing could be seen of his hair, since above the browline his head was swathed in bandages, but his sweeping mustache and pointed beard were brick-red. His bandaged left hand appeared to be shy a couple of fingers; nonetheless, he handled his reins skillfully and sat his big gray horse with the unconscious ease of the born horseman.

Milo tried a quick scan of the herald's surface thoughts, finding them as open and friendly as the merry green eyes. But there were other thoughts, too, and had been since first the freckled one had clapped eyes on Aldora. A glance at her showed Milo that she had read those thoughts as well. The trace of a smile pulled at the corners of her mouth.

The herald thrust the ferrule of his lanceshaft into the loam, dismounted gracefully, and strode to stand before Milo. He first bowed, then executed an elaborate salute. At closer range, Milo was aware of the copious perspiration coursing down the freckled face, the clenched teeth, and bunched muscles of the jaw.

"He is in pain," Aldora mindspoke rapidly, "intense pain. But he'd die ere he betrayed it, Milo. He is a fine young man, honorable and very proud."

Milo smiled. "Now that the formalities are done with, young sir, will you not sit and have wine with us?"

Tomos Gonsalos, despite his obvious thirst, sipped delicately at his wine. Savoring it on his tongue, he graciously complimented it, the silver cup in which it had been served, and his host and hostess, like the gentleman he gave every appearance of being. He had brought an invitation from King Zenos, who would share his evening meal with High Lord Milo, High Lady Aldora, and their four gentleman-captains. King Zenos stated that, aware as he was that certain deceased members of his House had established a reputation for treachery, his guests had his leave to ride with a bodyguard contingent of any size they saw fit. His intent, he emphasized, was honorable, but he wished his guests to feel secure in their persons.

After an hour's light conversation and another pint of wine, Tomos indicated that he should return and announce their acceptance of King Zenos' invitation. Upon rising, however, he staggered, took no more than two steps toward his horse, then crumpled bonelessly to the sward.

Aldora was kneeling beside the herald ere anyone else had hardly started forward. Expertly, she peeled back an eyelid, then announced, "He's burning with fever. One of you ride and fetch a horselitter. Someone help me get off his cuirass . . . but gently, mind you. He may have other hurts not so apparent."

Tomos did. High on one hip, an angry, festering wound sullenly oozed with pus and serum. It had been amateurishly bandaged, and friction against the high cantle of his warkak had torn the cloths loose.

A nearby bodyguard blanched and touched fingers to his Sun charm. "And he rode in here smiling, he did! How could he even bear to sit a horse?"

Herbuht Mai said, "A lifetime of self-discipline and generations of breeding . . . that, and ten leagues of pure guts. Yonder, trooper, lies a *man!*"

Bearing Tomos Gonsalos' white-pennoned lanceshaft, Milo paced his palomino stallion, unchallenged, into the outskirts of Zenos' camp. The camp was about as he had expected: under makeshift shelters, agonized men groaned and writhed; the air was thick with flies and heavy with the nauseating miasma of corruption and death; off to one side, an officer in hacked armor hobbled about, supervising the digging of a long mass grave and piled corpses patiently awaited its completion. A question put to this officer elicited directions to Zenos' "pavilion."

Outside the mean little tent, Milo slid from his kak and paced to the entry. Two tired-looking pikemen barred his way and politely asked his name, station, and business.

When Milo told them, their eyes goggled and the one on

the right gulped, then bawled, "*Komees* Greemos, please, my lord; *Komees* Greemos . . ."

A noble-officer limped to the entrance. The smudges under his eyes were nearly as black as the eyes themselves, and his bruised and battered face was lined with care and exhaustion. Although Milo had never seen the mountainous man, he well knew his reputation as strategist, tactician, and warrior.

"I am Milo, High Lord of Kehnooryos Ehlahs, Lord *Komees*. I come in peace. Please announce me to King Zenos. I would speak with him on matters of great urgency."

Milo felt instant liking for his young adversary. Zenos stood as tall as Milo, a bit over six feet. His eyes were brown and his gaze frank and open. His thick glossy hair shone a rich, dark chestnut, and his face was smooth-shaven. From what he knew of the young monarch, Milo would be willing to wager that he had had far less rest than any one of his remaining officers, yet he appeared as fresh as if he had but arisen from twelve hours' sleep. The grip of his hard, browned hand was firm.

"You are most welcome, Lord Milo." He waved his guest to one of the three seats—upended sections of sawn log, bark still on—that surrounded a battered, lightly charred field table.

Once seated, Milo got to the point of his visit, disregarding polite protocol. "Your herald, Tomos Gonsalos, lies in my pavilion. His wounds are grievous and he is being tended by the High Lady Aldora, who possesses certain wisdoms and skills in healing."

"Poor, brave, loyal Tomos." Zenos slowly shook his head. "God grant that he lives, for there are too few of his kind in my kingdom. "Would that I had not had to send him, hurt as I knew him to be, but it would not have been fitting to send a common trooper to issue my invitation to you and the High Lady, my lord. Tomos is my own cousin."

"Where," Milo asked, "are your *fohreeohee*, your *eeahtrosee*? Men who've fought bravely deserve professional tending. And what in Sun's name happened to your camp and baggage? My captains all assure me that there was no sack."

Standing near the entrance, *Komees* Greemos growled

deep in his throat and commenced to mumble a litany of curses.

Zenos cracked his knuckles. "I will be candid, my lord. Toward the end of the battle, certain of my mountaineer irregulars withdrew . . . rather precipitately. There was no rout, you understand, they are all brave men; but their loyalty was to me, personally, and some fool convinced them that I had been slain. It was they who sacked the camp, stole what they fancied or could carry, and burned the remainder. They slew every man who tried to restrain them or who got between them and anything they wanted. My pavilion alone they spared, but I had it dismantled and recut to make flies and bandages."

"Yes, a commander's first obligation is to his men," Milo said in agreement. "Would you accept the services of my *eeahtrosee*, those of them who can be spared from treating our own wounded?"

Komees Greemos limped over. "And what concessions will be required in return?" he snapped.

Milo looked up into the hulking nobleman's cold stare. "None," he said flatly. Then he added, "However, I would like to instigate a series of conferences with His Majesty and his council. Let me make it clear, however, that the offer of medical assistance is not contingent upon any other of my plans. I simply dislike to see good fighters suffer and die needlessly."

Zenos' brown eyes had misted and, though his features remained fixed, his voice quavered slightly as he once more gripped Milo's hand. "Two generations of my house have died fighting you, my lord, so probably shall I; but I shall never forget this act of unexpected generosity. Of course I accept, and I pray that God bless you.

"As for a conference with me and my council, that will be easy enough. Of the original council, only Greemos, here, and *Thoheeks* Serbikos are left; all the others fell in battle, as befitted men of their caste. Serbikos and his lancers are presently out foraging, but he should be back well before night, and we three can meet with you at your convenience. Can we not, Greemos?"

The officer shrugged his massive shoulders. "Whatever my

King wishes." He turned again to Milo. "How many armed men are coming with your *eeahtrosee*, my lord?"

Milo ignored Greemos' open hostility. "Not a one, Lord *Komees*. I had supposed that your army had sufficient hale men to give them what workforces they might require."

Greemos bobbed his head shortly. "Yes, that we can. I add my thanks to those of my King. I, too, want living, healthy troops, rather than corpses and cripples; we'll need them when next we battle your armies."

King Zenos looked appalled at this open threat in the face of unasked-for generosity. But Milo chuckled good-naturedly.

"You're nothing if not blunt and honest, Lord Greemos. I wonder not that Herbuht Mai spoke so highly of you."

There was an almost imperceptible thaw in the *Komees'* manner. "The gentleman-captain is a good officer. He is just and honorable in his dealings, and the provisions he set for the truce might have been much harsher. He is a worthy foeman, my lord."

The first meeting took place three days later at Milo's pavilion. King Zenos arrived, flanked by the dark, hulking *Komees* Greemos and by a freckle-faced, gray-haired officer who looked like an older version of Tomos Gonsalos.

Milo had brought along Herbuht Mai, of course, since he alone seemed to be able to get civil speech from the grim Greemos, as well as Guhsz Helluh. He had deliberately excluded Aldora. He had seen her disrupt more than one otherwise peaceful conference, and the combination of her vitriolic tongue and Greemos' pugnacity might well precipitate another pitched battle—something both he and Zenos wished to avoid. His other two captains were camp and perimeter commanders of the day, respectively. He had requested Captain of Physicians Ahbdool to attend for a specific purpose.

With wine served and amenities observed, Milo began. "King Zenos, Captain Ahbdool and his staff would like to bring the bulk of your more seriously wounded into my camp to continue treatment. For one thing, my camp is on higher ground and, consequently, healthier; for another, such an arrangement would immensely ease the tasks of the *eeahtrosee*, who must now spend much of their day in transit from one camp to another. Besides, we're better supplied—in all ways."

"Only," snapped Greemos, "because we presently lack the forces to raid your lines of supply. But these wounded of ours, what would be their status? Prisoners? Hostages?"

"Recuperating soldiers," Milo quickly answered. "They'll be free to return whenever they are fit and wish to do so. They'll be lodged in the same tents with our own wounded and all will receive equal food and treatment. Their friends may visit them and you and your officers may inspect at will."

"At whose will?" demanded Greemos. "Yours or ours?"

All had, at the beginning, been granted leave to speak freely, regardless of rank, and old Guhsz Helluh now took advantage of this privilege. Standing and leaning across the board, he growled, "At whose leave do you think, you noble jackass? This is supposed to be a peaceful conference, but you're trying to make it a nitpicking contest! If all you can think of is fighting, let us go outside and get a couple of pikestaves. Then I'll show you how we deal with oversized, underbrained windbags in Rahdburk!"

Greemos' big hands sought the hilts of the sword and dirk that Milo had wisely suggested they all leave on a chest near the entry.

A third man arose. Ahbdool was as large as Greemos and his flowing white robes made him appear even larger. A deep but gentle voice boomed softly from his barrel-chest, and his Merikahn was accented, for he was a native of the Black Kingdoms, where other languages were spoken.

"Noble gentlemen, before you go about making more work for me, please aid me in undoing some of the damage you have already wrought. Your Majesty . . ."

"Shut your thick lips, you lowborn black ape!" snarled Greemos, now fully aroused. "One more word from you when your betters are talking and . . ."

"Strahteegos *Komees* Greemos," began Captain Mai, formally, "with the exceptions of your King and Lord Milo, no man here is the peer of Captain Ahbdool. Despite his humility, his father is none other than the *Khaleefah* Ahboo of Zahrtogah."

"Pah!" snorted Greemos. "What does that mean to a northerner, black or white? You all breed like rabbits."

Guhsz Helluh chose to re-enter the fray, teeth and claws bared. "Yes, you buggering Ehleenee bastard, we do have large families. But that's mainly because we devote our amatory practices exclusively to women, whilst you perverts waste your seed on boy-children and goats!"

And so it went for some four hours more. All in all, Milo was not displeased with the outcome of this first conference. Most of the camp gained some diversion from the pikestave duel between Greemos and Helluh, which dealt neither any serious hurt and gave each a healthy respect for the other. It was agreed that the wounded would all be concentrated at Milo's camp; and Ahbdool was even able to persuade King Zenos to set about moving his own camp to a higher, more healthful location. The next conference was set for a week later. But it was fated to come much sooner.

3

The first to see the ship was a stripling of Clan Kuk, whilst descending the precipitous path from plateau to beach. Sacred Sun had but barely risen and the night mists still lay thick upon the tidal estuary. The lad first heard the rhythmic *clock-clock* of oars against tholepins. Then the sharp prow of the long, low vessel nosed out of the opaque whiteness. She was painted a dull brown-black, some ninety feet long and something under twenty feet in beam. Her two masts were unstepped and lashed into crutch-shaped forks. She seemed some huge bug, walking across the water on her twin banks of slender oars.

By the time Djahn Kuk of Kuk had scratched together a force of warriors and maiden-archers, got them armed and mounted, and gained the edge of the plateau, the intention of the shipmaster to ascend the river was plain.

An old chieftain shook his grizzled head. "It's not one of God-Milo's boats, that's for sure, and it's like to no merchant ship I've ever seen."

"No," agreed Kuk of Kuk. "I think it's one of the raiding boats from the Pirate Isles—the Sea Isle Ehleenee. I've never seen one, I admit—for some reason, they never raid Kehnooryos Ehlahs—but I've heard them described right often. Well, if they try attacking this plateau, they'll wish they'd stayed out on the Great Ocean!"

He swung about in his saddle and addressed his eldest brother, Pawl, Tanist of Kuk. "Ride back and blow the war horn. Send a man up the tower to light the signal beacon.

20

Get the old and the young, the sick and the kittens into
the fort, along with all the herds that can be quickly gathered.
Send half the warriors and maiden-archers to me and the rest
to the fort. And send me any cat that isn't nursing a litter,
too."

Rahn Duhklus of Duhklus was one of the first to join the
Kuk, heading a dozen and a half riders. The deep-throated
lowing of the great horn was still moaning the length and
breadth of the plateau, while clouds of dust were beginning
to rise into the lightening sky. The men at the river's edge
could not see the first flash of flame from the fort's highest
tower, but when the dense column of sooty smoke mounted
upward it was visible to all.

The Duhklus growled impatiently, fingering his dirkhilt.
"We should send riders to warn the inlanders; the Dirtmen
aren't as well able to fight for themselves as are we."

"Send horsemen through ten leagues of saltmarsh?" replied
the Kuk. "That ship could be to Kehnooryos Atheenahs, ere
our riders reached solid ground. No, and besides, where
there's one of those bastards, there's usually more. With most
of our young warriors and the largest part of the Cat Clan on
campaigns, I'll not countenance any more weakening of our
defenses, Tribe brother."

"And, look, you." The Kuk swept his arm to the northwest, where a thin line of black smoke was rising against the
blue sky. "The Goonahpolisee have seen our beacon. The
capital will be alerted soon enough."

High Lady Mara Morai, Milo's wife and presently ruler of
Kehnooryos Ehlahs, as well as commander of what troops
were left in the garrisons of the capital and its port, was upon
her morning ride. She and her retainers were combining the
exercise with some desultory hawking when they saw a rider
coming, hell-bent, across the fields.

The full-armed *kahtahfraktos* drew rein before her and
saluted quickly. He was streaming sweat and dust-covered
and his mount was flecked with foam and shuddering with effort.

"My lady, the Lord Hamnos prays you return at once. A
pirate bireme from the Sea Isles has come up the river and

would dock at the port. It is said that the Sea Lord himself is aboard and he seeks audience with the High Lords."

Mara was glad that she was seated when the old *Neea-heearkos*, Lord Petros, officiously ushered in the three visitors. She hardly noticed the two older strangers, but mere sight of the youngest man sent gooseflesh over every inch of her skin, and a glance at one of the side mirrors showed that her face had visibly paled.

"Lekos!" she breathed, more to herself than to anyone else. That face was his, and each line of the slim, whipcord body, even the pantherish grace of his movements, were those of the young Alexandros of Pahpahs. Eighty long years of life had not erased her love for him, she now realized. She loved Milo, but not, she admitted, as she had loved Lekos. But she had no more time for musings, for old Petros was speaking.

". . . felt that these matters were of such urgency that he himself embarked to inform the High Lords. His ship has sailed or rowed night and day and entered the river at dawn. I thought it best that it be moored amongst the Fleet, since some merchants are known to bear ill will toward the Lord of the Sea Isles and his captains."

At this, there was a tittering in the gathered throng and the two older seamen laughed openly. Mara noticed that even the younger man allowed himself a wry smile . . . and that smile, too, was of such old familiarity that it sent a pang through her heart.

Three hundred years of life had at least granted Mara instant control of her emotions. Her face a mask, she nodded. "You have done well, Lord Petros. The strangers may be presented to me."

The court herald banged his staff, bellowing, "Now comes Alexandros, Lord of the Sea Isles."

He announced two other names, but Mara did not hear them. *Alexandros,* she thought. What other name could such a one bear? I *saw* him slain, forty years ago, and he then an old man past sixty. Yet, here he stands before me, that same young man I loved . . . and who so loved me . . . eighty years in the past. How is such a thing possible?"

The two older seamen knelt, but the younger one bowed formally from the waist—the obeisance due to one equal in rank. When he spoke, his voice was deep and rich, but so, too, had been that of the earlier Alexandros.

"My Lady Mara, often have I heard your beauty praised, but lavish as was that praise, my own eyes now tell me that it was an unforgivable understatement."

"Young lord," she replied, "your compliment was most gallantly couched and much appreciated. But my curiosity has become aroused. No one of your people has visited our shores—professionally or otherwise—for at least forty years. What now brings you to our court?"

Alexandros took a step forward. "My lady, I bear urgent intelligence for the ears of the High Lords alone. I must speak with them . . . and that soon!"

Mara shook her raven tresses. If no one else had informed him, she might as well do so; he'd know soon enough. "Lord Alexandros, my husband, High Lord Milo, the High Lord Demetrios and his wife, the High Lady Aldora, are all on campaign. I hold the Confederation in their absence. We four are all equals in rank and power, so you may deal with me as you would with them."

Shortly, he bobbed his head. "Very well, my lady. But I know something of courts. I would speak what I know only to you. These captains will corroborate my words."

Mara ordered the reception hall cleared, then thought more deeply and led her guests down a side corridor to a small, windowless, thick-walled room. *Neeaheearkos* Petros and his squad of marines had followed and would have entered, but she forbade it.

Petros reddened, expostulating, "But they still are armed, my lady. You should have guards, within as well as without."

Mara laughed and laid one slim hand on his arm. "You forget, old friend, steel cannot harm me. And I feel Lord Alexandros to be an honorable man. If you wish to serve me, have wine and fruit and cheeses fetched. You have done well today."

When all were seated and refreshments were placed on the table and the door was securely bolted, she took a chance and addressed the young lord telepathically. "Do you mindspeak, Lord Alexandros?"

He answered her in the same manner. "Of course. No one

who cannot can hold high rank among us. It is the way we communicate with our orks, much as do your people with their cats."

"Then I propose we converse in just this way, since even the stoutest of doors and the thickest of stones may develop ears on occasion. But we four are not the only ones here with mindspeak talents, so maintain your shields against all save short-range, personal contacts. Now, what is this earthshaking news, Lord Alexandros?"

While sipping at his wine, the young man's mind said, "We have . . . contacts among the swamp and fenfolk of all coasts except yours. In return for immunity from raids, as well as a bit of hard money now and then, they keep us informed of such matters as vulnerable towns, movements of patrols and warships, sailing dates of worthwhile merchant ships—things of that nature."

Mara nodded. It was reasonable that, over many generations, professional marauders would have built up such a network of agents.

Alexandros went on. "Throughout the last five years, we have generally avoided the coasts of the Southern Kingdom. With the dynastic struggle ongoing, every city, town, and village that wasn't a blackened ruin was an armed camp. Stray detachments of troops were tramping hither and yon over the countryside, at little or no notice, and it sometimes seemed that every headland concealed a warship or flotilla. The Captains' Council decided it was just too risky."

"But I'd heard that the war was all but over some six months ago," Mara said.

"True," commented Alexandros, assuring her. "The new High King is Zastros of the House of Zladinos, a most ambitious man, it would seem."

"Since when," interjected Mara, "has the usurper of the Southern Kingdom become a *High* King?"

Alexandros grinned. "Since Zastros had himself crowned such, my lady. As I said, he is a very ambitious man.

"At any rate, when we heard of the end of the civil war, two biremes were dispatched to nose along the coast to see what they might and re-establish relations with any of our former informants who might remain. Captain Yahnekos, here," he said, gesturing toward the dark-visaged, hook-nosed man to his left, "captained one ship and Captain Van-skeleeg"—this time he nodded at the graying, fair-skinned man on his right, who was cracking nuts in his big, square, tar-stained hands—"the other. Why don't you tell the High Lady how the voyage went, gentlemen?"

"Well," began Captain Yahnekos, "we slipped through the shoals by night, and by dawn we were sheltered in a little overgrown cove what's nearly a lake at the ebb. To see it from a-sea you wouldn't think a damned pirogue could get in nor out; but, unladen, a bireme can. I've used that cove quite often over the years . . two full fathoms up to ten foot of the shore in most places, a sweet-water spring no more'n two cables' length inland. I come on 'er meself, y'know, more'n twenty year ago, an' . . ."

Captain Vanskeleeg shoved aside a heap of nutshells. "Your pardon, my lady. Yahnekos, here, is a first-rate captain, but if he fought the way he talks, he and his company would all be sharkbait long since."

"We laid up in his cove the full length of a day, put out men to watch the sea and sent patrols inland to some swamp-men's villages. Not a single sail was spotted that whole day long, not even fishing craft. It looked like we had the only two ships on that whole stretch of coast.

"But when the patrols come back, it's a different pot of fish. Both of the villages was part burnt and looted and the swampers what wasn't dead was scattered to hell and gone. Aroun' night, an old swamper—name of Pinknee, who'd been one of our men there—come down to the cove. He said soldiers had been scouring the swamps for nigh on a month, not slavin', though, impressin' for the fleet an' the army. All they was takin' alive was strong, hale men an' boys an' oncet they'd got 'em chained up, they'd kill every oldster and child they could get a spear into . . . and after they'd done with the women, they'd kill them too, even the good-lookin' ones, by damn!

"Anyhow, seems old Pinknee's village had just been hit that mornin'. He never did say how he come to get away, but he did tell us how we could cut off the soldiers what done it. We talked it over and decided we owed it to the swampers and, besides, it sounded like fun. We hit 'em whilst they was makin' nightcamp, kilt an hundred an' six pike-pushers an' one officer. We persuaded the other officer"—the captain's thin lips split in a wolfish grin—"that it might be to his best interests to tell us why he was 'pressin' the swampers, what town he and his troops was from, an' how strong the garrison was. After he'd told us ever'thin', we give him to the swampers.

"So, anyhow, we come to find out that ol' Zastro'd pulled all but six score of the garrison outa Sabahnahpolis—that's a middlin' size town, a tradin' town, just inland of the swamps. Town's on a bluff and has good walls. Some swampers say it'uz builded on top of what useta be a God-town, but that don't cut no bait fer us. We'd alluz been scared to tackle'er afore, but we worked us out a plan.

"We put chains on mosta the swampers, but so they could shed 'em easy like, y'see, and they all strapped dirks an short swords under their shirts. We figgered Yahnekos looked more like that Ehleenoee officer'n me, so we put that fancified cuirass on him . . . and was that a job, my lady; big as his ol' belly is, we had to lay him down and set two *big* men on top of the breastplate afore we could get the thing buckled!"

Both Alexandros and Vanskeleeg grinned hugely, while the thick-bodied Yahnekos glared at them from under lowered brows and muttered something obscene under his breath.

Vanskeleeg continued. "So we got an hundred-odd of our reavers into the pikemen's gear and, along about dusk the next day we marched up to the landward side of Sabahnahpolis. They'd closed the gate, o'course, it gettin' toward night an' all. You should'a heard ol' Yahnekos, though—sounded just like one of them nobles, he did! Said he'uz tired and needed him a wash, an' if they didn' get them gates opened afore he'd took another breath, he'd have ever' manjack's parts off an' feed 'em to his hounds.

"Well, the gate opened up and we marched in and it was a bad night for Sabahnahpolis, it was. After we'd killed all the gate guards, we headed for the river gate to let in the shipload of reavers an' swampers what had come upriver in my ship an' Yahnekos'. We come to the marketplace and here sat this fat man in gold armor on a big, pretty horse. Behind him was what looked like five hundred pike-pushers and we figgered we'd fought our last fight, but we charged 'em, anyhow. But it turned out they was nothin' but merchants and wharfmen and factors and such like, all dressed up in old armor. They didn't know one end of their pikes from t'other, an' when it looked like they might have to *use* them over-growed spears, they throwed 'em away and scattered.

"Well, our boys killed as many as they could catch, and ol' Yahnekos, who was still aboard the horse, went after the feller in the gold armor an' he damn near lost him, too, an' I can't but feel sorry for them two poor horses with them two tubs o' blubber a bouncin' and a jouncin' . . ."

"Enough, you red-faced pig!" Captain Yahnekos slammed a hard hand upon the table. "*You* call *me* garrulous, yet you've strung a short tale out over the best part of a quarter hour."

He addressed Mara. "My lady, my captive proved to be the Royal Governor of Sabahnahpolis, one Daidos. At his order, the city stronghold was opened and, when we'd disposed of all the garrison, Daidos showed us to the treasure that made our voyage so profitable—thirty pounds of silver coin and nearly twelve pounds of gold, taxes and excise monies destined for the capital.

"Our boys gleaned a good bit more from within the town, then took time to knock down the main gates and smash in all the boats, after driving every horse they could find into the swamps. Slows up pursuit, that does.

"Daidos told me that he could bring a goodly ransom from his king or his family, so I had him put in Captain Van-skeleeg's forepeak, as it's bigger than mine. I'd taken a fancy to Daidos' daughter and Vanskeleeg to some merchant's spawn, so we let the boys grab some wenches to keep them happy on the return voyage and pulled out for the Sea Isles." He showed strong, yellow teeth in a crooked grin.

Alexandros took over the narrative. "By the time I first interviewed Governor Daidos, he was in poor shape, both physically—he'd never been to sea before, and a bireme is not the most comfortable of ships in a rough sea—and mentally. He spoke to me without attempt at prevarication, as one Ehleenoee gentleman to another. He told me that he had lied to Captain Yahnekos. His family had been impoverished by the civil war and he knew his king to be far too busy with certain plans to see to the ransom of one minor official. In return for his life, he pledged upon his honor and the honor of his house to impart to me information that could very well save my kingdom. His words had piqued my curiosity, so I agreed not to kill him if his story proved true.

"Daidos said that all the ships of the Eastern Fleet and a third of the Western Fleet were assembling at *Neeaheeopolis*, their great port just north of the Death Swamp, which separates the Southern Kingdom from the Witch Kingdom. Meanwhile, Zastros is gathering a huge army, calling troops from as far west as the Ocean River. After five years of a kingdom-wide war, you know that his realms must be aswarm with veteran soldiers, and Zastros is offering them anything that he feels might tempt them—amnesties and lands to nobles who fought against him, manumissions to escaped slaves, excellent wages to mercenaries, and mountains of loot for all. And they're flocking to his standard in droves. A week before his capture, Daidos had reliable word that Zastros already has near one hundred twenty *thousand* men! His cavalry alone number some forty thousand, and he has five hundred armored war carts, each drawn by a pair of North-horses. Too, he has units of another animal—I cannot now recall what Daidos called them—the description of which he gave sounds like a huge, deformed boar. If he wasn't exaggerating, they are more than three meters high, have four legs as thick as trees, tushes as long as a tall man, and a long nose that drags the ground but is flexible as a snake and can be used to throw darts or stones or slash with a three-meter sword blade! Sounds utterly fantastic, does it not? Yet Daidos swears it all to be true."

Mara nodded slowly. "Such beasts do exist in the Southern Kingdom, Lord Alexandros, though I was not aware they had been trained or adapted for war. In our language they are called 'elafahsee'; the aboriginals call them 'eluhfuhnts.' The kings of the Southern Kingdom have been breeding them for centuries. I saw their herd about a hundred and fifty years ago."

She regarded her wine for a moment, then added, "I would

suppose that Kehnooryos Ehlahs would be the logical objective of Zastros' hosts, since we have already subdued most of Karaleenos."

"Yes, my lady," said Alexandros. "But he harbors more grandiose schemes, as well. His fleet is to pace his army up the coast, going up navigable rivers to assist his land force where necessary. They intend to bottle up your fleet in this river and capture the ships, unharmed. if possible.

"When Kehnooryos Ehlahs is taken, Zastros will send his fleet to try to storm the Sea Isles or, failing that, blockade us and starve us into capitulation. Obviously, the madman has never seen the Sea Isles and has but scant information concerning them. Our central lagoon and its islands are impregnable. There is but one narrow, twisting channel from the sea; otherwise, our seaward coast is an unbroken ring of cliffs—jagged, precipitous cliffs, my lady, the very lowest being twice the height of this city's wall. They constitute natural fortifications and, in the few places skilled climbers might come up, we have added stretches of crenellated wall and certain other refinements.

"If he thinks to starve us out, he and his fleet have a longer wait than I think they can afford. We have little arable land and grow little food, but for that very reason our storehouses are always stuffed to bursting. Beside which, the lagoon is usually full of fish.

"No, my lady, my kingdom and I have precious little to fear from any number of Zastros' men or ships, but you and yours will be hard-pressed to overcome the host he is gathering. I command forty-three biremes and a handful of sailing-merchantmen fitted with sweeps, a total force of near five thousand of the fiercest fighters in the world."

"And you want to cast your lot with Kehnooryos Ehlahs?" Mara was genuinely puzzled. "But why? Why to many things, Lord Alexandros? Why did you undertake so long and difficult a voyage for the sole purpose of apprising us of our peril? Why would you now risk your ships and your men in our behalf?"

Alexandros refilled his goblet and leaned back in his chair, stretching his long legs before him. "That, my lady, is a long story. but I'll tell it, that you may know that honor of my house and not avarice impels my offer.

"It began forty years agone, when your clansmen and allies were threatening this city and realm."

4

Lady Mara's messenger—a subchief of Clan Morguhn—pounded into camp in mid-afternoon of the fourth day after the first conference. Milo had the message in mindspeak—always quicker and more detailed than oral communication—and then turned both horse and rider over to Captain Ahbdool. The little man and his great-hearted mount had done better than a hundred miles a day!

Milo gathered his four captains and gave them most of the news; their individual reactions were about what he would have expected of them.

"God-Milo," the Maklaud immediately mindspoke, "let me send riders to *Ehlai* and to the west. That will give us at least twenty-five hundred warriors; also, if we can boat the elders and the children up to Kehnooryos Atheenahs, I can almost guarantee nearly thirty hundred maiden-archers and matron-archers."

Captain Zarameenos cracked his knuckles. "Irregular cavalry and horse-archers are all very well for raiding and scouting, even for flanking a host, under the proper conditions; but we'd best leave the mountains for later and get the main army down here. It takes time to move forty-thousand men."

"Precisely," stated old Guhsz Helluh authoritatively. "I estimate that your army will need two weeks to reach us; but for the most part, they will be marching on good roads through friendly lands. Think, man, think how much longer it will take to move three or four times that number of fighting

31

men. *Plus*"—he tapped the table for emphasis—"their baggage, artificers, seige train, and the vast rabble of noncombatants that always follow a large host. His force is far too large to make much use of the trade road; they'll mostly have to move cross country, and unless they know the country or have damned good guides . . ."

Herbuht Mai groaned. "All right, Guhsz, so they'll take four, maybe six, weeks to reach our current position. But how could anyone stop them when they do get here, eh? One hundred twenty *thousand* fighting men! By my steel, there aren't that many men in Pitzburk and Harzburk combined!

"Middle Kingdoms' rulers think Lord Milo powerful because he can field an army of fifty-thousand-odd. But how can he or anyone stand against a force of nearly three times that number?"

Captain Zarameenos had never really liked Mai. "If you're afraid to die for the realm that pays you, mercenary, why didn't you stay in the same barbarian pigwallow that spawned you?" he sneered.

Both Helluh and Milo tensed themselves, ready to try to prevent bloodshed. The Maklaud eased backward and slyly loosened his saber, hoping to get at least one swipe at that strutting Ehleenee bastard before the northerner slew him.

But Mai's good sense prevailed. He was far slower to anger than Helluh. "Captain Zarameenos," he replied slowly, carefully choosing his words, "I am certainly as nobly born as are you, possibly more so, but that is of no moment in this place and time. I do not fear death; indeed, He and I have brushed one another countless times on many a field. I well know, as do all my Freefighters, that wounds or death is the certain fate of most of us, but we continue to practice our highly dangerous profession because it is the only one most of us know.

"The nobility of your Ehleenoee realms are usually highly educated and, early on, are habituated to a soft, pampered life of culture and books and soft music and luxurious palaces and pleasures that men like me cannot understand. Consequently, few of your peers made decent soldiers.

"I dislike you probably as much as you dislike me, Captain, but I'll gladly give any man his due; you are the rare ex-

ception to most of your ilk—admirable strategist, able field
tactician, an officer who obviously cares for the welfare of his
men and willingly devotes time to seeing to that welfare.
Were any large number of Ehleenoee nobles the fighting men
that *Strahteegos* Gabos, *Komees* Greemos, and you are, you'd
have scant need to pay out your gold to the Freefighters you
hate and despise!

"In the Middle Kingdoms, Captain Zarameenos, a nobleman begins his war training at the age of seven or eight. At
fifteen or sixteen, if he's still alive and uncrippled, he's a seasoned veteran and he spends the best part of however much
life is left him in making use of his hard-learned war skills—
either for his home state or for foreign states. Yes, he fights
for gold. Who can live without gold? If he's lucky and a good
leader, he manages to recruit a condotta, equip it, and hire it
out as a unit for what must seem tremendous amounts of
money to some. But, Captain Zarameenos, damned few con-
dotta-captains die wealthy, not if they're all they should be,
for more than nine-tenths of the hire of their services goes
back into the men for whom they are responsible."

"Captain Zarameenos," barked Milo, "you owe Captain
Mai an apology."

"Yes," agreed the blackhaired officer, "I do, especially
since most of what he said is true. As a class, my peers have
become too soft, too civilized. Furthermore, most of us know
it and despise ourselves because we are not the men that our
ancestors were, so we have to hire men of the kind we should
be to protect us. Something, Lord Milo, *must* be done to
change this pattern."

Milo nodded. "Something will be done . . . if the realm
survives what's coming. Captain Maklaud, I want ten of your
best riders and twenty-two of your strongest, swiftest horses.
You and the ten will ride within the hour—no armor, no
bows, no spears, only saber, dirk, and helm. You and the
men report back here.

"Captain Mai, as soon as I've dispatched the messengers,
you and I will ride to King Zenos' camp.

"Captain Zarameenos, have a detachment of your artificers
determine how long it would take to partially or completely
render the bridge unusable.

"Captain Helluh, delegate your command to a good officer, then strip to sword and dirk and helm and take my stallion and a couple of good remounts. I have a very important mission for you; a man of lesser rank or experience couldn't carry it off."

Something over an hour later, Milo sat cradling his goblet, his booted legs thrust out before him, hoping that he had made the best decisions. If he had, many thousands of men would die before autumn. If he had not, there would certainly be years of untold misery and suffering and death up and down the much-altered Atlantic coast of what had once been called "North America." In his case, nearly a hundred years of hopes and dreams and plans would be dissolved into nothingness. All that he and Mara and Aldora could do would be to go back to the Plains, where still roamed clans of Kindred, or take ship and wander the world as he had done alone for almost two centuries.

He ticked off his accomplishments: the Maklaud and two others to Lord Gabos with the main army in the western mountains. The *Strahteegos* was ordered to patch up some sort of truce with his opponents—a loose alliance of rapacious mountain tribes, as prone to fight each other as anyone else—break camp and march directly to Kehnooryos Atheenahs by way of Theesispolis, whose garrison of Freefighters he was to absorb. At the capital, he was to reform so as to include all the troops Mara had been able to scrape together, then join Milo with all haste.

Two clansmen had ridden directly for *Ehlai* with the message for the Kuk to boat his noncombatants to the protection of the capital's walls, then to ride with every man and woman who could sit a horse and swing a blade or pull a bow, as well as every adult prairie cat, battle-trained or not. Old, crippled, or nursing cats were to guard the herds.

The other five clansmen had ridden to five of Zenos' former cities that Milo knew to have fairly large garrisons to bid those troops join him by the quickest possible means.

Guhsz Helluh was pounding toward Kumbuhluhnburk, the most southerly of the Middle Kingdoms and long an ally of Kehnooryos Ehlahs. He bore authorizations to recruit any and all condottas—either horse or foot—that he could contact. Price haggling was to be kept to a minimum and Milo had repeatedly emphasized that quantity was of far more importance than quality in this case.

He had sent Aldora and her bodyguard to the capital. For all her failings, the girl was a damned good administrator, and Mara was sure to need her.

With dark approaching, Milo had sent a lancer ahead to advise Zenos that he and Mai were coming. It would help no one to have Mai killed by an overalert sentry. Consequently, they were met at the south end of the bridge by *Thoheeks* Serbikos and an honor guard of his Karaleenos lancers, who courteously escorted them to the hilltop where Zenos' new and larger tent—a loan from Milo—had been erected. There waited King Zenos, hulking *Komees* Greemos, and the savory smell of a roasting boar, which Greemos had singlehandedly slain near the river.

As he swung from his saddle, Milo bluntly said, "Your Majesty, gentlemen, I bear tidings of great import to us all. I suggest we talk first, then dine . . . if anyone still has an appetite."

When Milo and Mai had finished, there was a moment of silence as their listeners digested the shattering news. Then Greemos glared hatred at Milo, snarling, "It's all your fault, you damned, unnatural barbarian upstart! If you hadn't set your mind to annexing the best part of our lands and driving us to the wall, none of this Zastros business would be happening. If I thought I could kill an unholy thing like you, by Jesus, my steel would be in your guts this minute!"

King Zenos pounded his fist on the table, his face dark with anger. "Enough, enough, damn you for a fool, Greemos, *enough* I say!" When he had the silenced *Strahteegos*' attention, he snapped, "We've no time for name-calling or blame-laying or digging into old wounds; I, at least, recognize the facts that my late father and I and you but inherited the certain results of my grandfather's greed and duplicity; he left Kehnooryos Ehlahs no choice save to neutralize the threat Karaleenos constantly poised under him.

"But this is the dead past. We must look to the future, and there will be no future—for any of us—if we fail to stop

King Zastros, which we cannot do if we do not stand as one with Lord Milo. As of this moment, we are allies. Now, have the meal served. After that, we'll discuss strategy and I'll give my orders to you and Serbikos."

By noon of the following day, the scanty Karaleenos baggage was trundling north across the bridge. Shortly they were followed by columns of tramping infantry, a smattering of cavalry, and a few mounted officers.

Young King Zenos had taken a hundred lancers and ridden south and west, into the mountains to assure his kinsmen—both his mother and his grandmother had been the daughters of the chieftains of powerful mountain tribes—that he was alive, to alert them to the approaching danger, and prepare them for the hordes of lowland refugees who would shortly seek sanctuary in their domains. He and Milo had agreed that the mountain warriors could be of more military value if they remained in or near their home ground nibbling at Zastros' western flank, retarding his advance with harassing raids, picking off stragglers and scouts, even ambushing smaller units . . . anything to buy a little more time.

Greemos and a score of officers had taken detachments of cavalry south and east to warn the inhabitants of cities and towns and villages to take livestock and valuables and flee to the mountains, after burning all standing crops and destroying foodstuffs and supplies they could not take away. If the huge army could not subsist on forage, more strain would be placed upon Zastros' lines of supply, which might buy precious time.

Thoheeks Serbikos, his officers, and the bulk of the cavalry had fanned out northward on a far more delicate mission. They were to contact the leaders of the various Karaleenos resistance movements in the territories Milo had conquered, explain the present danger, inform them of their former sovereign's alliance with the conqueror, and urge them not only to refrain from rebellion upon the withdrawal of Milo's garrisons, but to form themselves into units, arm, and march to swell the forces now assembling to repel King Zastros' horde.

Zenos, Milo, and all the senior officers had agreed that their present position was as good a defensive site as they might find. At this point, there was a bare forty miles of plains between the saltfens and the mountains. The River Luhmbuh in itself presented a formidable barrier—for almost all of the forty miles of lowland, it ran both wide and deep, with but the one bridge spanning it. Miles upstream were a couple of fords, but they were said to be narrow and treacherous at best and could be easily defended by small forces.

Milo put the most of his forces and those of his new ally to vastly enlarging the camp and to making a true, palisaded *castra* of it—the artificers laid out and marked the courses of the huge rectangle, and then the troops were set to digging the ditch that would front all four sides. Milo put even the wounded to work, whittling points onto wooden stakes and making caltrops, then dumping their handiwork into old latrines to "season."

The spoil from the ditch—twenty feet wide, ten feet deep—was mounded inside the enclosure and, held in place by forms made of split logs supported by stakes, tightly packed. And the work went on by day and by night. Other troops spent their days in a forest, half a mile to the north, felling trees and transporting them to camp, where the artificers topped them and shaped the trunks and larger branches. The tops were denuded of leaves and small twigs by walking-wounded and the tip of each and every remaining branch was given a sharp point—dumped in embankments or lashed together, these would make quite an effective abatis.

After a week, armed men began to trickle from north, west, and south: some were mounted; most were afoot; a few were disciplined Freefighters; the rest were straggling bands gathered together by one of Zenos' officers, some noble or a village headman. One and all were immediately attached to one of Milo's or Zenos' units and put to work on the fortifications.

When a Freefighter officer grumbled within Milo's hearing distance that at least some time should be devoted to drills and arms-practice, the High Lord had the officers and nobles assembled before his pavilion.

"Gentlemen," he began, "we have perhaps a month until the south bank of the Luhmbuh will be aswarm with the largest single army these realms have ever seen. We mean to stop them there, on the south bank; but, if we fail, if those rapacious hordes manage to fight their way onto this side of the river, we must have a stronghold that can be defended by a minimum number of troops, while the bulk of the army withdraws northward. This stronghold must be so situated that the enemy will feel impelled to attack and overwhelm it. Ours is so placed, straddling as it does the eastern trade road, menacing the enemy's lines of supply. Additionally, the *castra* must be strong enough to hold off as many troops as possible for every possible second.

"Now, I know that many of you professionals are somewhat incensed at the lack of unit drills, field maneuvering, and arms-training for the volunteers."

There was a grumble of assent from among his listeners. He raised a hand to still it.

"As for unit drills, I doubt not that every Freefighter and Confederation soldier in this camp could perform them in his sleep . . . and probably often has," he added with a grin, drawing answering grins, nods, and a few chuckles from the throng.

"As for training the volunteers, most are ill armed and we have scant equipment to supply them and, even had we mountains of arms and armor, one bare month is just too short a time to teach plowboys to angle their pikes and stand firm in the face of a cavalry charge.

"As for field maneuvers, they are totally unnecessary, since I have no intention of engaging Zastros' army in formal battle. Hopefully, by the time his army comes up to the Luhmbuh, we will have sixty thousand troops here. King Zastros' will outnumber us by more than two to one—not impossible odds if we wage purely defensive warfare, but sheer suicide for most of us if we allow ourselves to be lured into a formal engagement.

"Do not misunderstand me, gentlemen, I mean to fight! I mean to send the scattered remnants of King Zastros' army running back southward as fast as their legs can carry them. But, gentlemen, I mean to fight at a time and place of *my* choosing. The place is here, if we can hold the river line long enough; the time is when the odds are a little more in our favor.

"And they will be, gentlemen, can we but hold our place for a maximum of eight weeks from this day! The Duke of Kuhmbuhlun is making ready to march with his entire army and that of his cousin, the Count of Mahrtuhnburk. By now, Captain Guhsz Helluh should be ensconced in Salzburk recruiting every uncommitted Freefighter within sight or hearing distance. We are in alliance with the Lord of the Sea Isles and he has agreed to furnish an unspecified number of fighters. And I received, less than an hour ago, a message that the King of Pitzburk is dispatching five hundred picked noblemen and six thousand dragoons, as well. He also assures the Confederation of financial assistance.

"So, you see, we are not alone, we are growing stronger, gaining more allies every day. All that we need is a little more time. I think that what we are doing here will buy us that time. But I must have the active support of you gentlemen to accomplish my plans."

A short officer shouldered his way to the front, respectfully removed his helm from his grizzled head, and politely asked, "Can I be heard, Lord Milo?"

Milo stepped aside, making room on the earthen dais and the heavily scarred, one-eyed veteran joined him, walking with the rolling gait of an old cavalryman.

"I be Senior Lieutenant Erl Hohmun, of Mai's Squadrons. I ain't no gentleman, less you consider the youngest son of a younger son of a younger son such, so don't nobody expec' me to talk like one. But I've fought for Lord Milo's gold for more'n thirty year now—I'uz a trooper under ol' Djeen Mai, a sergeant and senior-sergeant under his son, Bili Mai, and now I'm servin' Djeen's grandson. In all that time, I ain't never seen High Lord Milo lose a battle, ain't never had to retreat from any set-to that he himself planned. Ol' soljers, like me, can feel things in their bones, an' right now I got me a strong feelin'. If we all stick by the Lord Milo, do ever'thin' he tells us, an' do it *his* way, we'll still be a-lootin the Southern Kingdom, come this time nex' year!"

A roar from the Freefighter officers was taken up by the Confederation professionals and, seriously outnumbered, the nobles could only join in. Milo could have hugged the ugly little one-eyed Lieutenant Hohmun, who in a few short, blunt

words had saved the day for him and Kehnooryos Ehlahs
through assuring him of the overwhelming support of the of-
ficer-corps. Milo had tried to appeal to such things as reason,
honor and self-sacrifice . . . and never aroused any real en-
thusiasm; the gap-toothed dragoon, at least seven hundred
years Milo's junior, had won them with those two basic things
for which soldiers fought in this savage world—leadership of
a proven and undefeated lord, and loot.

Milo said a few closing words, called forward and introduced some recent arrivals, then dismissed the formation.

Maxos and Beros, both petty nobles of the Karaleenos city
of Thalasopolis, who had grudgingly brought in what was to
have been a band of anti-Confederation guerrillas, strolled off
hand in hand, Maxos hissing, "But, darling, it was so *obvious*,
to an intelligent man, at least. The High Lord had that disgusting barbarian creature *planted* . . . probably spent just
days drumming those exact words into the little ape. . . ."

Not being mindspeakers, neither had a mindshield, so Milo
was easily able to eavesdrop on their thoughts; those two
would possibly bear watching. But their type was a very small
minority; most of the departing nobles and officers radiated a
new sense of purpose, expressions of dedication and loyalty
and dreams of gold and women of the Southern Kingdom.

Milo could but wish that he felt as confident of victory.

5

At his own suggestion, Lord Alexandros had remained in Kehnooryos Atheenahs when his captains and ship returned to the Sea Isles. He informed them that he was hostage to their full cooperation in the effort to stop King Zastros.

Despite her burning curiosity regarding the young man's relationship to that man he so closely resembled—his namesake, the late Lord *Strahteegos* Alexandros of Pahpahspolis—Lady Mara could find no time for her hostage-lord for over a month, so filled were her days with the multitudinous chores engendered by her responsibilities. Nor, despite Milo's gesture of solicitude, was Aldora of any immediate help. Without even reporting to Mara upon her arrival in the capital, she dismissed most of her guard, ordered a barge, and had herself rowed downriver to *Ehlai*, not returning until all the Tribe's fighters had departed and the young and old were being boated up to Kehnooryos Atheenahs.

Nonetheless, Mara did the best she could to make the Sea Lord's stay a happy one. Gooltes and Manos, his two body-guard-servants, were augmented by a host of skilled slaves and a detachment of Lady Mara's own private guard.

At the end of the first week, Lieutenant *Komees* Feeleepos, the detachment commander, reported to his mistress.

"My lady, Lord Alexandros makes friends quite easily. Indeed, I have come to admire and respect him . . . not that my personal feelings would in any way impair my loyalty to Your Grace, of course," he added quickly.

41

"Of course." She nodded. "He mixes well, then, with the court?"

The corners of the young officer's eyes crinkled with his smile. "Oh, yes, my lady. He has received invitations to nearly every noble house in the city. Some, he has already accepted; five, he has attended."

"Whose?" demanded Mara. "And what transpired?"

"*Theftehrah*, it was dinner with Lord *Neeaheearkos* Petros and some of his officers. They spent most of the evening discussing the sea, the various coasts, ships, fleet tactics, plus navigation and other mysteries. To my thinking, Lord Petros still doesn't quite trust Lord Alexandros, but he now has respect for his skills and experience . . . he might even like him, in time.

"*Treetee* was a dinner party at the town house of Lord *Vahrohnos* Paulos of Notohpolis . . . the Vahrohnos' usual variety of party, of course."

Mara's lips wrinkled in disgust. She had always found it difficult to be even marginally polite to High Lord Demetrios' coterie of pederasts; but she had tried, mostly for the good of the Confederation, since many of them were powerful nobles and/or high-ranking and efficient officers. She had suffered many crushing disappointments in her long, long life; but, considering all that Alexandros' name and physical appearance meant to her, she was fearful of asking her officer that question she knew she must. Trying desperately to mask any evidence of her inner turmoil, she inquired, "And how did Lord Alexandros enjoy the party?"

The lieutenant chuckled. "The Sea Lord wasn't born yesterday, Your Grace. He obviously knew his host and fellow guests for just what they were. When he was offered the so-called place of honor—sharing Paulos' dining couch—he very politely requested a chair, instead, saying that he suffered indigestion if he dined other than erect. He ate and drank and chatted in a most friendly fashion with all who addressed him. He lavishly complimented his host's home, decorations, food, wines, and musicians; but he appeared to be completely unable to comprehend the meanings of a number of quite overt verbal overtures that the *Vahrohnos*, who seems rather taken by him, put to him. When the feasting was done and

Paulos announced that the 'entertainment' was about to commence, Lord Alexandros rose, pleaded fatigue, thanked the *Vahrohnos* for the dinner, and we took our leave.

"I am reliably informed that, immediately subsequent to our departure, Lord Paulos threw a knife at one guest who made some comment or other, bashed in the front teeth of a second, then burst into tears and fled the dining hall."

Mara felt as if the weight of a war horse had been suddenly lifted from her. She smiled broadly. Then another thought came to her and she frowned.

"Be very careful of the *Vahrohnos* and his clique, Fil, warn Lord Alexandros to be equally cautious. That kind of man can be petty and spiteful as an unpaid whore, when balked; furthermore, *Vahrohnos* Paulos is a veteran warrior and a duelist of some note, should he take it into his head that he has been publicly humiliated and decide to force Alexandros into a death match. Well, things could get very sticky with the men of the Sea Islands should any harm come to their Lord."

Feeleepos smiled lazily. "Your Grace need have no fears in that direction."

"Oh, I know," said Mara impatiently. "You and your men will protect him from assassins, but if Paulos opts to call the Sea Lord out, man to man . . ."

"In the unlikely event, my lady," he said, interrupting, "my money will go on Lord Alexandros. Have a death match between Paulos and Alexandros, and they'll be putting a well-hacked buggerer in Paulos' family tomb the next day! Believe me, my lady, I am a professional. I have seen the *Vahrohnos* fight and I have seen Lord Alexandros fight and . . ."

"When," snapped Mara, her eyes flashing fire, "have you *seen* Lord Alexandros fight, Lieutenant?"

The officer squirmed under her glare. "My lady, Lord Alexandros spent his first two days touring the city, but on the morning after the *Vahrohnos'* party, he said that he felt in need of some exercise. I took him to the main guard barracks, thinking that he might wish to swim or run or jump or throw spears, but he insisted that we stop at the practice yard, where he first requested, then demanded, a padded

brigandine, weapons, and shield. What could I do, Your
Grace? I had him fitted out with regulation training weapons
and a full-face, double-thick helm. Then I warned the weapon
master that if any harm came to Alexandros, I'd have off
his ears and nose.

"Well, they whacked away for a while, Weapons Master
Rahn taking more blows than he gave. Then Lord Alexandros spun around and stalked over to the barrier where I was
standing. He said that he had come for a practice bout, not a
sword dance, that he'd rather fight me than old Rahn, and
that I had better give him a real fight or I'd shortly wish I
had."

Mara could almost hear the quoted words, for they sounded so like that other Alexandros, that long years' dead
Alexandros. "And you fought him . . . *really* fought him?"
she prodded.

Feeleepos nodded gravely. "Yes, Your Grace, I really
fought him, and I pray that I never have to face him in actual battle. My lady, he is of slight frame and build, as you
know. He was burdened with a thick, hot brigandine that
reached to his knees and weighed exactly twice as much as a
scaleshirt, ten pounds of helm, and double-weight infantry-
style shield and sword; yet he danced around me like a cat
toying with a mouse, a thrust here and a hack there, a slash
at the legs, and a split second later a stab at the eyes. By
straining every muscle, I was able to catch or deflect them all
with either shield or sword; but when he shouted his war cry
and closed with me, Your Grace, there was no way I could
have stopped him. Then he stepped back and saluted me and
thanked me for my efforts.

"Of course, a crowd of off-duty officers and men had
gathered around to watch; we don't discourage the pastime,
for observation, too, is a form of training. At any rate, Lord
Alexandros pulled off his helm and asked if any of the onlookers would care to give him a bout. When no one immediately came forward, he suggested that the swords be tarred
and offered a silver piece for every tar mark an opponent
could put on him.

"With my approval, the weapons master took him on . . .
and lost. Then he took on two other officers and a dragoon

sergeant of the Harzburk Ambassador's retinue. When he finally tired and took off his brigandine and helm, there was not one speck of tar on either!"

Mara shook her head in wonderment. "What did this champion, after all that?"

"He threw spears for a while, and then we had a swim. And he's like a fish. I've never known a man who could swim so far under water!"

"How did he spend that night, Fil?" Mara was again friendly, her worry erased. "Another banquet?"

"No, Your Grace, he said that he felt like having a quiet evening. We dined in his suite, played *zahtreekeeohee* for a while—he checkmated me quickly, two out of three times, and I'm not sure but that he allowed me my own win—and then we simply sipped wine and talked."

"Of what did you and he talk, Fil?"

"Of so very many things, my lady, that I hardly know where to begin. He asked many questions concerning the court—who were the leaders and principal members of the various cliques, which cliques favored which high lord or high lady, the names of the most powerful men, and what were their vices or weaknesses. He asked many questions concerning our customs, not only of the court and palace, but of the city and countryside. He had me tell him all I knew of the Horseclans. He asked me to tell him of my hereditary city and lands, of my boyhood, of my campaigns and the different tribes I had fought, of my service and duties and various assignments since I entered Your Grace's guard, of my future plans, of my hopes and aspirations. He dismissed me near midnight."

"What did he do the next day?"

"*Pemtee,* he arose and broke his fast early, then spent the entire day, until sunset, in the palace library. My lady must, I fear, ask the librarian what Lord Alexandros read, for I assigned some guards and went about other duties of mine."

Mara shrugged. "I can't see that what he read is of import. And what of that night?"

"Dinner and entertainment at the palace of Lord *Strahteegos* Gabos." The young officer grinned wickedly.

"Yes." Mara cracked a knuckle. "I heard of that rout. Two

duels came out of it, one a death match. And what sort of swath did our Sea Lord cut through the ranks of the grass-widows?"

"Lord Alexandros could have had any woman in that palace, Your Grace, merely by a nod or a look or a crook of one finger. The Lady Ioanna never took her eyes off him from the moment he arrived. In the course of the evening, she and a number of others managed to corner him, and the language used in some of their invitations would have embarrassed a stone statue!"

"And his replies were . . . ?" prompted Mara impatiently.

"The essence of diplomacy, Your Grace, and if he was dissembling, he hoodwinked everyone . . . including me. His tale was guaranteed to touch the heart of almost any living female. He declared that, soon after his arrival, he had seen the woman of his dreams, had fallen in love with her at a single glance, but could not declare his passion, as she was the honorable wife of a powerful lord. He admitted that, though he might never be enabled to consummate his love for her, his needs must await the improbable chance, since the charms of no other woman could any longer stir him.

"My Lady, they all wept for pity of his plight; a few swooned. When the tale got about the gathering, Lord Alexandros was put to a merciless questioning to establish the identity of his love, but he simply answered all with a sad smile and a shake of his head. I think that each of the ladies offered at least once to plead his case, if he would but tell her whom to approach; several of the gentlemen suggested that there were numerous persons in the city who, for a modest fee, could quietly and discreetly dispose of inconvenient husbands . . . permanently. He refused them all.

"Naturally, the 'entertainment' had been going on about us from the end of the last course. We drank a bit more wine, and Lord Alexandros chatted with some of the spectators, but when they brought out the trained animals, he indicated his desire to leave and we did so, being unable to locate our hostess."

"I cannot imagine where Lady Ioanna could have been," remarked Mara sarcastically. "She's like the Confederation Army—open to any man between fifteen and forty. I don't know why Gabos hasn't beaten her to death long since. An occasional affair when a woman's husband is on a long campaign is one thing, but she's put so many horns on poor old Gabos' head that I fail to see . . . but it's none of my business."

"Well, what did our guest today, Fil?"

"Over to the barrack-yards again, Your Grace. This time, though, he had to offer gold to get bouts from any, save old Rahn and me; soon, I may have to start assigning men to fight him. Another thing—he wants someone to teach him to ride a horse. He says they have no horses in the Sea Isles."

Lord Djeree Pahtuhr was a horseclansman. Though he hardly looked his age, he had been born on the high plains, thousands of miles to the west, on the very year that the tribe commenced its twenty-years-long migration, which had ended in the conquest of Kehnooryos Ehlahs. He had fought in every battle of the conquest and in many thereafter. Now, most of his hair was gone and precious few strands of red adorned what little remained, but his eyes still sparkled clear and blue as a mountain lake. Nor had sixty years bent his back, stooped his shoulders, or weakened him. Though short and slight like most of his race, he stood straight as a spearshaft and, though his clasp of greeting was gentle, Lord Alexandros could sense the formidable strength in the old man's hand.

Horseclansmen, the Sea Lord discovered, were as blunt and informal as were his own people. Truly revering only their Undying God and two Goddesses—Milo, Mara, and Aldora—they considered all others—kings, nobles, even their own chieftains—as mere men and treated them as such.

"You tell Mara that I'll be right glad to teach the young feller to ride," Pahtuhr told Lieutenant Feeleepos. "Though it ain't much teachin' to ridin', mostly, it's fallin' off 'til you get the hang of how to stay on."

He turned to Alexandros, looking him over critically. "Can you mindspeak?" He asked it suddenly and silently.

"Yes." Alexandros answered just as silently.

"You sure can, an' strong, too; not too many of you Ehleenee got that much power—them what can mindspeak, a-tall. That's good, what with that an' your build, I'll have you finished in no time."

High Lord Milo's breeding farm lay some miles northwest of the capital, so Djeree had a pair of huge, white mules harnessed to an old-fashioned war cart. When the slave-driver was in place, he and Alexandros mounted, whereupon the slave lashed the mules to a fast trot, able to maintain such speed in the city only because he drove the Military Highway, just inside the city walls. Lord Djeree was apparently well known and popular with the soldiery, for many an arm was raised as they passed and many a ribald greeting shouted.

They never even paused at the west gate and the sparse traffic scurried from their precipitate progress. Then the driver put the team into a ragged gallop and the heavy, springless vehicle jounced and clattered. The slave seemed to know every boulder and pothole in the seldom-used road, and at least one wheel seemed to make violent contact with each imperfection.

But Alexandros adapted, guessing that the relaxed, expressionless old man was putting him to some test. Facing forward and taking a firm grip of the brass side rail, the Sea Lord put into play the muscular harmony and sense of balance that had kept him erect on the steering deck of many a storm-lashed bireme . . . but he still felt that his every tooth was being jarred from his jaws.

Lord Djeree's hand on the driver's arm ended the hell-ride at the first milestone. The mules were reined up to a smooth trot and the slave adeptly avoided the rougher areas of the roadway.

Grinning broadly, Pahtuhr clapped a horny palm onto Alexandros' shoulder. "Ever'thin' I've heard about you, is true, boy; you got balls; an' no mistakin'. Me an' Feelos, here, we done had many's the high-mucketymuck Ehleenee a-screamin' his head off and a-bawlin' his eyes out long afore we come to the milestone. You sure you ain't got no Horseclans blood, Alex? You're built like it, though you're some taller."

The Sea Lord shook his dusty head. "No, Lord Djeree, I am a *Kath'ahróhs*—pure Ehleen—according to my late father."

The old man scratched his scarred, sun-browned scalp.

"Well, with your guts and your build and strength, and your mindspeak, you'll be a fine rider in record time."

Milo's herd was one of his experiments. The plains horses, on which the Horseclans had trekked to the east, were brave, intelligent for their species, and possessed a well-developed capacity for mindspeak; but they were slight, wiry, and small, like the race who had bred them. A large plains-horse stallion might be expected to stand fifteen hands at the withers, but the breed averaged considerably less.

The eastern breeds, especially those of the Middle Kingdoms, were all rolling muscle and tremendous power, some weighing twice as much as a plains horse. Pitzburk, Harzburk, Szunburk, and most of the other northern states would not even give war training to an animal of less than seventeen hands. Such horses easily bowled over the mounts of Horseclansmen, who quickly discovered that the only way they could stop a charge of *Kahtahfraktoee* or dragoons was by a concentrated arrow-rain at a distance, breaking up and slowing the formation before it reached them.

But the clansmen considered the majority of the eastern horses stupid, and not without some justification; furthermore, few possessed more than rudimentary mindspeak. Although larger, eastern horses were far less hardy and self-sufficient than plains horses and were subject to a plethora of diseases and infirmities without a maximum of human care.

During the conquest of Kehnooryos Ehlahs and in the ten years following, a certain amount of uncontrolled interbreeding had taken place as captured eastern animals were introduced into plains horse herds. Then, thirty years of controlled interbreeding was instituted by Milo at a number of farms scattered about the Confederation.

The herd from which Alexandros was to be mounted was small, less than two hundred horses; but they were the best of the best—combining the finest qualities of eastern charger and plains horse.

Lord Djeree, using only mindspeak, introduced Alexandros to the king stallion, informing the big, glossy bloodbay that Alexandros, too, was a king as well as a seasoned warrior. The king stallion and the two men then strolled through the herd, mindspeaking those of their host's choosing. Finally, they selected a young, war-trained stallion, solid black with three white stockings. The three-year-old and Alexandros stumbled into immediate rapport and, when the man had given the horse a mental picture of the speed, ferocity, and awesome power of the huge, shiny-black Orcas, the black happily accepted the name "Ork."

Lord Djeree's predictions were well proven. Alexandros spent most of the next two weeks at the farm, at first under the old man's expert tutelage, then alone with Ork. When he, Feeleepos, and Lord Djeree trotted their mounts through the west gate, toward the end of the Sea Lord's third week in Kehnooryos Ehlahs, no onlooker would have thought but that he had been a horseman from boyhood.

Although he had, of course, quartered a sextet of guardsmen at the farm and made occasional visits, Feeleepos had spent most of his time in the palace. Like any palace, Mara's swarmed with informants, but under his stiffest questioning, none would admit to having heard *Vahrohnos* Paulos refer to Lord Alexandros in any stronger terms than "a silly, fickle boy." The two guests Paulos had assaulted after Alexandros' departure had both armed and ridden south, apparently fearing King Zastros' army less than the *Vahrohnos'* disfavor. Nor could underworld contacts in the city learn of any plot to poison or assassinate the Sea Lord. Paulos' actions—or, rather, lack of actions—had both Feeleepos and Mara puzzled and deeply worried when the hostage-lord rode back into the city.

After a long, hot soak and bath, Alexandros dined in his suite with Feeleepos and Lord Djeree, then tossed the dice with them for an hour, glad when he lost a dozen gold pieces to the old man, since the horse master had refused any recompense for the long hours of extra labor. After a last goblet of wine, he bade them both good night and retired.

Lord Alexandros awakened from a sound sleep with the certain knowledge that someone was within his bed-chamber. His every sense straining, as he lay immobile, he thought he detected a brief rustle of cloth, then knew that a pair of unshod feet were slowly shuffling toward him from his right.

Tensed for action, he kept his eyes shut and his body still as death until he could feel that the presence was standing by the side of his bed. Gradually opening his eyelids, he could see a man-shaped form, black in the dim starlight that filtered through the windows.

Lacking a weapon, he suddenly spun on his buttocks and lashed out with a sinewy leg at the midsection of the feature-less bulk. Hardly had his foot met flesh, bringing a grunt of pain and surprise, than the agile man was out of his bed, firmly grasping a pair of thickly muscled shoulders and slam-ming a knee up between two hairy thighs. His antagonist wheezed another breathless grunt, followed by a shrill, womanish scream. Alexandros gave the man a firm shove backward, then leaped for the wall, where hung his sword.

But ere he could draw his steel, the room began to fill with guards. Their torches and the quickly lit lamps revealed to all the unenviable condition of the intruder . . . and his identity.

The clothing and sandals of Lord *Vahrohnos* Paulos lay on the floor near the door. Paulos himself, nude, sobbing, and glistening with the sweat of agony, lay curled in a knot, clutching his groin and retching onto the tiles.

"Shall we slay him, Lord Alexandros?" inquired a sergeant. "Or take him downstairs and lock him up?"

"Is he armed?" Alexandros questioned.

The suffering noble was roughly stretched out and his clothes were examined, but no weapon was in evidence.

With the help of two guards, Alexandros got Paulos onto his feet, guided the stumbling, gagging man out onto the bal-cony, and pitched him over the low balustrade. As Alexan-dros recalled, it was a fall of less than six feet . . . with a thick hedge of roses for a fall-breaker.

But when Feeleepos arrived and learned of the Sea Lord's disposal of the intruder, he was quietly furious.

"By every known god, my lord, you should have slain the bastard on the spot! You had every right to either gut him yourself or let the guards spear him; after all, he was not here by your invitation. Was he, My Lord?"

"No, good Feeleepos, he was not. But there was no weapon on him, so I don't think he meant me harm."

The lieutenant savagely struck his own forehead with the

heels of his hands. "My lord, the alliance of your people and ours could mean a great deal to both, but what do you think will be the reaction of your captains if we have to report you slain? The Lady Mara and I have been twisting every tail in the palace and city to ensure that you stay alive and unharmed. Even should he decide to not hire a poisoner or assassin, your uninvited guest is a well-known warrior and an infamous duelist. His temper rests on a hair and he has been known to force men to a death match, simply because he fancied they were thinking insulting thoughts of him!

"No, my lord, Paulos didn't come here to kill you. He bribed a couple of my guards and came in to either seduce you or rape you, whichever tactic he found necessary. He has been known to do such before, though never to a royal guest. I feel the man to be deranged, but that makes him no less dangerous.

"Had he died in this room, it could have been quietly forgotten. As it is, as Your Lordship has handled it; the very least we can expect is a challenge."

Lord Alexandros yawned widely. "Feeleepos, I greatly appreciate all that you and the Lady Mara have done. I also appreciate your worry for me. But rest your minds, please. I do not fear the Lord Paulos on a personal basis—had I, I would certainly have slain him as he lay helpless before me. If he demands a fight, I will meet him. Tell my captains that I died in a duel and there will be no recriminations. The duel is far more common amongst my people than amongst yours.

"Now, if you will excuse me, I would like to sleep for what's left of this night."

6

For three days Lady Mara and Feeleepos walked on eggs.
The two guardsmen who had taken Paulos' bribes expected a
flogging. It did not come; they were simply sent south with
an infantry unit . . . as common pikemen.

When the challenge came, it was delivered to Alexandros'
suite by two whom he remembered from the *Vahrohnos'* banquet. As he recalled, the heavyset man with the black
mustache was one Shaidos; the slender, lisping one was called
Hulios.

Alexandros had been riding that day and he and Lord
Djeree and Feeleepos were dicing when the new guard first
announced the names of the visitors, then admitted them.

The Sea Lord remained seated, as the two offered short,
perfunctory bows. Shaidos spoke: "Lord Alexandros, we two
gentlemen are here to present the honorable challenge of the
Lord *Vahrohnos* Paulos of Notohpolis. He . . ."

"Is it not customary," snapped Alexandros coldly, "for a
challenger to present himself in person when the challengee is
of higher rank?"

Shaidos flushed with anger. "I have endeavored to be civil
to you, but I am a nobleman of Kehnooryos Ehlahs. I'll hear
no prating of custom from the lips of a common pirate!"

Feeleepos started forward, but Alexandros restrained him.
Smiling lazily, he remarked, almost conversationally, "Lord
Shaidos, you have just insulted my rank. These gentlemen
beside me bear witness to that fact and to the additional fact
that I hereby issue challenge to you. You may, of course, set

53

time and place and weapons, but, if it suits your fancy, I'll be happy to engage you after I've finished with the *Vahrohnos*. He does want to fight, I hope. Or are you two simply scouting out my suite for another of his midnight incursions?"

Shaidos' flush deepened. "I accept your challenge, but I don't think you'll be able to meet me. Lord Paulos has suffered injury and deep humiliation at your hands, and he insists that you fight him to the death."

Alexandros waved a hand airily. "Oh, very well, I accept your master's challenge. I'll even excuse his absence; as I recall, he was neither walking or talking very well when last I saw him."

Lord Djeree snickered loudly.

"According to the Code," announced Shaidos, "you have choice of time, place, and weapons."

Alexandros nodded. "Armor will be helmets and scaleshirts; it's easier to swim in scale than in plate."

"Sw . . . *swim*. . . ?" Shaidos stammered.

"Yes, swim, to keep from drowning," Alexandros answered. "Go and tell your master the time is in three days on a raft moored in the main channel of the river. Tell him that, as weapons, I choose boarding-pikes."

"But . . ." began Shaidos, "that is not a gentleman's weapon. I mean, Lord Paulos will never accept . . . I mean, it is a waste of time to . . ."

"Go and tell him, I said!" roared Alexandros.

It was a very hot, humid day. Anyone who could stayed indoors, but not Shaidos and Hulios. Alexandros toyed with them for hours, keeping the two scuttling between the palace and the mansion of the *Vahrohnos* until they were both wringing wet and drooping.

Each of his suggestions of time or place or weapons was geared to bring instant rejection from the peacock-proud *Vahrohnos*. Feeleepos, after his first shock had abated, grinned almost constantly, while Lord Djeree all but rolled on the floor in his mirth.

When, in late afternoon, the two emissaries plodded back into Alexandros' suite, they were limp with exhaustion. Their hair, so carefully curled and draped on their first visit, hung dull and lifeless. Their copious sweat had washed the last trace of cosmetics from their faces.

"Lord Alexandros," said Shaidos hoarsely, "my lord declines to engage you in the manner you last requested. His refusal is in honor, as butchers' cleavers are not the weapons of gentlemen."

Alexandros had tired of the sport. "When push comes to shove," he said gratingly, "*gentlemen* fight with any weapon they can lay hand to. But I will relent, I will give the *Vahrohnos* what he wants. So hear my stipulations well.

"I will meet the *Vahrohnos* at the second hour after dawn in three days. I will meet him in the practice-yard of the guard's barracks. My attendants will be Lord Lieutenant Feeleepos and Lord Djeree Pahtuhr. Armor will be plate cuirasses, studded leatherkilts, plate greaves, and open-faced helms. Weapons will be three-foot bucklers, and one dirk, in addition to the sword. The sword is to be no more than one hand wide, nor six hands long; your standard-issue infantry sword would be a good choice. Think you that your overly choosy master will accept *these* terms?"

Shaidos cleared his throat. "I am certain that he will, sir. I set identical conditions for our own meeting . . . if ever it comes to pass."

Alexandros smiled coldly. "It will, little bumboy, it will. Have no fear."

Though cloudy, the morning was bright. Duels were supposedly a private affair, but news of this one had traveled widely, for Lord Paulos had many friends . . . and twice as many enemies. The yard was a frequent setting for duels, many of them as well attended as this one promised to be, so the guardsmen had set up the wooden bleachers and awnings the afternoon before; by dawn, every inch of board had been rented, and the guards were dragging stools and benches from their barracks to seat latecomers. . . at an exorbitant price, of course. Rumors that High Lady Mara was in attendance passed through the throng, but since all the ladies were heavily veiled, there was no certain knowledge. Guardsmen passed through the throng as well—a few hawking cool wine and sweet meats and heavily salted biscuits, most engaged in making bets on one contender or the other.

Within the yard, Feeleepos and Djeree reported back to Alexandros after examining Lord Paulos' gear and weapons. "His cuirass and greaves are fancier but of no better quality. He had a nasal on his helm, but we made them remove it. There is a springspike in the boss of his buckler and the iron rim is knife-sharp all around. You should make him use another. . . . You can, you know, under the Code."

"The men of Kehnooryos Makahdohnya often carry shields like that," replied Alexandros slowly. "No, I'll not protest. Let him bear that shield. Perhaps I can show him a pirate trick when I've tired him enough.

"What of his sword and dirk?"

"I don't think his dirk blade is envenomed, Alex." Djeree grinned. "But I pissed it down from one end to the other, just for luck."

Now Alexandros knew what had prompted the angry shouts at the other end of the yard. It was well known that somehow urine would cleanse most poison pastes from steel. But to imply that someone like Lord Paulos might bring a poisoned dirk to a duel . . .

"And what was the outcome of that little episode, Djeree?"

Still grinning hugely, the old fighter shrugged. "I'm to meet him next week—if you leave anything of him. We're to fight with sabers, mounted."

"The sword Lord Paulos brought was a ground-down broad sword, the type they normally swing with two hands in the Middle Kingdoms; of course, the hilt had been shortened and the blade was the proper width and length, but the weapon was far heavier than yours, due to the fact it was half a finger thicker," stated Feeleepos soberly. "Djeree and I protested, naturally, and Captain Nathos backed us up after he'd swung and hefted it. So Paulos will be fighting with a regulation guard's sword, identical to yours, my lord."

The sun peeked briefly through the clouds as the combatants crossed to the center of the yard, where waited the senior-captain of guards, who had been agreed master for this duel. Behind him stood two archers, their hornbows strung.

Lord Paulos shone like a jewel as the sun sparkled on his

gold-inlaid armor. Alexandros' armor—chosen, like the rest of his panoply, from the main armory—was browned for field service, its only decoration being an abbreviated jet crest on his helm and the Three Orks of the Sea Isles copied onto the front of his cuirass and the face of his buckler by a palace artist. In the bleachers, Paulos' friends laughed and joked at the Sea Lord's drab appearance.

Senior-Captain Nathos bade them halt face to face and five feet apart, their attendant-gentlemen a few feet behind them.

"My Lord Alexandros, I will recite these rules mostly for your benefit. I am certain that *Vahrohnos* Paulos could recite them in his sleep, so often has he stood here. Since this is to be a death match, I'll not go into the signals for withdrawal. Much as I detest seeing Ehleenoee noblemen kill each other, it is not my function to attempt mediation of your quarrel.

"As this is to be a foot combat, signals will be by drum roll rather than bugle. At the first drum roll, you will each retire to your assigned place." Nathos indicated two squares of colored sand about ten yards apart. "There, each of you will be subjected to a last inspection, conducted by me.

"At the second drum roll, you will draw your steel, salute your opponent, and commence orders. Anyone who enters this yard before I do will be killed. The duelists will fight with the weapons they now bear and *only those weapons*. The sudden appearance of any darts or throwing-axes or spare dirks will earn their bearer an arrow; so, too, will the throwing of sand or dust into your opponent's eyes—this is not a general battle, but a duel. Do I make all points clear, gentlemen?"

Alexandros moved out slowly, his body half crouched and his eyes peering through a narrow slit between the iron rim of his buckler and the front band of his helm, for men had been known to throw a sword blade into an opponent's unguarded face and end a match before it had hardly commenced. Taking careful steps and circling, he and Paulos came very gradually to striking distance.

Surprising Alexandros with his speed, Paulos feinted a thrust at the same time his shield rim slashed at the Sea Lord's knees. Turning the thrust with his own blade, Alexandros took the slash on his buckler. The sharp edge cut through all three layers of tough hide to the wood beneath, bringing shouts from the crowd. Quickly recovering, Paulos drove in, trying hard for the face or throat, his own face and body behind his buckler.

Alexandros' shield came up, but then he abruptly straightened his left arm and slammed the face of the shield into Paulos' extended sword arm, aiming his iron boss for the wrist. He failed to strike the wrist or hand, but Paulos almost lost his sword, and the Sea Lord's thigh thrust penetrated leather kilt and flesh alike.

When Paulos skipped backward, he could be seen to favor his left leg and, while they maneuvered toward another meeting, a thread of blood crept from beneath the *Vahrohnos'* kilt.

Above the loud comments of the crowd, Lord Djeree's voice roared, "That's the way, Alex! Take his parts off next time, boy!"

But Alexandros was worried. Aside from involuntary grunts and gasps, his foeman had spoken not a word—no threats, no sanguinous promises, nothing. From experience, he knew a silent fighter to be among the most dangerous. Their first encounter had convinced him that if the big, brawny man was not his equal, he was frighteningly close. Taunting the *Vahrohnos* might not help, but it was worth a try—anything was at this stage.

"I've yet to hear your voice, you perverted ape," Alexandros sneered. "Or did my knee make a soprano of you?"

"No," Paulos growled, "but I mean to make a full eunuch of you . . . before I slay you. I hate so to waste beauty, you ungrateful young bitch, but I offered you my love and you answered me with hurt and humiliation; I must make of you an example."

"If you can," grated Alexandros.

Lord Paulos sighed. "Oh, I can, lovely Alexandros, I can. This is my thirty-seventh duel. But, I reiterate, I would prefer to not slay you, darling. If you'll, even now, say that you'll be mine. Let me draw a few drops of blood, and I'll declare the contest done and spare your beauty and your life. Please say yes."

"*Fagh?*" Alexandros spat. "I'd sooner couple with a sow.

And you had my answer one night last week . . . when you saw fit to sneak into my suite."

They circled and circled. Alexandros' battle-trained eyes told him that Paulos seemed less relaxed and supple than he had earlier. He hoped it was the tenseness of anger, but it could equally well be fatigue or the pain of the thigh wound, which had continued to slowly seep. He decided to try once more to arouse the *Vahrohnos* into a rash move.

Conversationally, he inquired, "Why do you duel so often? Duels are much more common in my realm than here, but I know of no man of mine who has taken part in so many."

"I am the Lord *Vahrohnos* of Notohpolis," stated Paulos, a bit pompously. "My sacred honor . . ."

Alexandros' barked laugh interrupted. "*Honor*? *You*? You High Lord of buggerers, you don't really know the meaning of the word. How could you, when your highest aspiration is to wallow in dung?"

Lord Paulos' face was now becoming darker and his jaws were working, so Alexandros threw a final verbal dart. "No, you piece of filth, you've slain your thirty-six men in an attempt to prove what no one can ever prove—that Paulos of Notohpolis is truly a man. Give up. No amount of blood will ever transform you into what you have never been, even the whore who spawned you . . ."

But he had no more time for words.

Paulos charged, flat-footed, his sword slashing before him. Alexandros danced lightly from the big man's rush, managing to sink a deep stab into the *Vahrohnos'* left arm, between epaulet and buckler. Roaring like a bull, Paulos whirled and slashed wildly, but his blade whistled through empty space. The Sea Lord had dashed behind, and his red-tipped sword again penetrated Paulos' shield arm, lower this time, near the elbow.

Shaidos and Hulios were screaming advice to the *Vahrohnos*, but their voices were lost in the constant shouting of the onlookers.

But it could not last. Paulos suddenly ceased his berserker tactics and, once more silent but for the ragged breathing caused by his exertions, recommenced his wary circling. There were two more brief flurries of swordplay, but the

Vahrohnos seemed to be much slower in getting up his buckler. And this was a mystery to none, for the entire left side of his cuirass was streaked and smeared with blood.

Alexandros decided to end it; after all, he had another duel to fight. He swept in, his thrust aimed low. Paulos' steel caught the thrust and the blades slid their full length, until crossguard met crossguard. While the thews of their sword arms strained, Alexandros slammed his buckler into Paulos' shield, his boss below the *Vahrohnos'*. For a brief moment, he feared that Paulos might fail to rise to the bait, but then he felt the shock of the barbed spike as it locked the two bucklers together.

Quickly, he jerked up on his buckler. Paulos was unprepared for such and his own sharpened rim gashed his chin deeply. He did the natural thing, taking a step backward, then another and another, trying vainly to gain room to disengage his sword, now that his locking device had trapped his opponent in a position where brute strength meant more than agility. But Alexandros doggedly followed, step for step, until Paulos' bloody cuirass was grating on the stone wall that separated yard from drill field.

For the first time, Alexandros discerned fear in Paulos' bloodshot eyes. Adroitly twisting his sword out of the engagement, so long maintained, the Sea Lord swung his body out as far as he could. He allowed Paulos to raise his blade above his head and start the vicious downswipe . . . and then he stopthrust him, his gory blade grating on the bones of Paulos' forearm.

"That was a pirate trick, Lord Paulos," Alexandros panted. "Now, with your help, I'll show you another."

Keeping the *Vahrohnos'* blood-gushing right arm skewered on the sword, Alexandros stepped closer and began to strain upward on his buckler, forcing Paulos' higher . . . and higher, as the weakened, throbbing left arm began to fail. The knife-edged rim of Paulos' buckler drew closer and closer to his own throat. Closer still, blood from his gashed chin dripped onto it.

When it was bare inches away, Paulos gasped, "My lord, please, I beg you!"

"Thirty-six men," hissed Alexandros. "Thirty-six slain, and how many more dishonored because they feared you?"

Up came the rim of the buckler, and so still had it become that they might have been alone. Up, closer, ever closer.

Tears joined the sweat pouring down Paulos' face. "As you love God, my lord, if you're going to do it, do it quickly! You have a sword. Why must you torture me so?"

Savagely, Alexandros jerked his blade from the useless right arm and Paulos tensed, then raised his chin. But the Sea Lord did not thrust. "As I recall, you intended to emasculate me ere you killed me. I am not so crude, but perhaps I'll take an eye or two. Eh?"

The cursive rim of the buckler was now pressed hard against Paulos' flesh. As the dripping sword point neared his eyes, he jerked his head to the side . . . and cut his own throat!

Paulos remained briefly erect, the two bucklers dangling from one limp arm. His lips moved, but only a gargling sound issued from him. Then his knees buckled and he pitched onto his face.

The cool, dry air of the guards' armory was as refreshing to Alexandros as a cool swim, after the mugginess and heat of the practice yard. Furthermore, its thick granite walls muted the laughter and shouted conversations of the crowd to a dull muttering, so that the long, narrow room seemed a place of peace, despite its rack upon rack of weapons.

The Sea Lord sat slumped in a camp chair, his cuirass replaced by a thick cloak, that he might not chill and stiffen, while Djeree Pahtuhr sponged his head and face with a mixture of warm water and wine. Feeleepos dragged over a low chest and lifted the young victor's booted feet, now filthy with blood and dust, onto its top, then started to unbuckle the greaves.

Alexandros opened his eyes, raised his head enough to see the officer, and shook it, saying, "No, Fil, leave them on. They don't bother me. And, remember, I've another match this morning. Don't let that sword I used get away, either; it's nicely balanced."

"Small chance of that, Alex," chuckled Djeree, whose

broad grin had never left his face since the gory demise of *Vahrohnos* Paulos. "I entrusted your steel to a couple of my lads to clean it and restore its edge."

Drawing up another chest, Feeleepos seated himself and commenced to knead the twitching thigh muscles of his charge. Djeree laid aside his sponge and applied his powerful hands to the neck, shoulders, and upper back. Since both were veteran warriors, they knew just where their ministrations would be most effective, and soon had their subject completely relaxed, his arms and legs no longer trembling.

There was a tentative rap on the heavy doors. Then one opened enough to admit one of the guards' officers. Feeleepos arose. "What is it, Stahvros?"

Smiling, the officer rendered Alexandros a formal salute. "My lord, that was a beautiful piece of work out there! I am sorry to disturb you, but another of the late *Vahrohnos'* pack is in the corridor. He demands audience."

When the doors were opened, in came Lord Shaidos, flanked by two men who had also been guests at Paulos' ill-starred party. The *Vahrohnos'* former second was very pale, his lips had become a thin, tight line, and a tic spasmodically jerked at his cheek. But Alexandros could detect no panic or fear in the black eyes, only a dull resignation.

Old Djeree straightened and chortled, "Hawhaw, Alex, boy, look who's come to try and weasel out!"

If the visitor heard Pahtuhr, he gave no indication of it, addressing Alexandros directly. "Lord Alexandros, I must confess that I was not expecting this outcome. I have sent some friends to my home for my panoply, but it may be as long as an hour before they return. If you wish to fight me immediately, however, it is your option; if so, sir, I am sure I can be fitted out from the arms in this room."

The Sea Lord shrugged and spoke in flat, disinterested tones. "Lord Shaidos, I'll not force you to fight with unfamiliar weapons. Take all the time you need or wish. Also, why don't we change our meeting to a blood match? I've no real reason or desire to kill you."

Shaidos' lips twisted wryly. "You are most magnanimous, sir, and I thank you. But, no, I'd as lief be dead as live in penury; you see, I wagered all I owned on poor Paulos."

The Sea Lord shrugged again, then pushed to his feet. "As you like, sir. But should you experience a change of heart, your gentlemen can find me in the guards' officers' baths. I feel the need for a hot soak."

As he walked toward the door, he heard old Djeree grate, "I'll expect my twenty-five hundred *thrahkmeh*s to be paid me *before* your suicide, lordy-boy Shaidos. I dislike collecting from widows!"

Once again, Senior-Captain Nathos soberly recited the rules and procedures, but added, "Lord Shaidos, I am informed that Lord Alexandros is willing to settle for a blood match. Is this agreeable to you?"

The gold traceries on Shaidos' enameled helmet flashed to the shaking of his head.

Nathos sighed. "Very well. You may retire to your squares, gentlemen."

Alexandros' doubts that the dispirited Shaidos would fight were speedily dispelled. The garishly attired man trotted forward at the first tap of the drum roll and, without preliminaries, launched a lightning attack, his sword a silvery blur.

The Sea Lord managed to catch or turn every slash and thrust on his target and sword blade, but the contacts jarred him to the very bone. Shaidos was obviously stronger than he appeared. Doggedly, he remained on the defensive, staving off attack after precipitate attack, knowing that his opponent must soon burn himself out—no mortal man could maintain such violent exertions for long.

And so it proved. Gradually, Shaidos' blows and stabs were delivered with less force, his foot and shield work perceptibly slowed. As the target involuntarily fell enough to disclose his strained, streaming red face, Alexandros stamped into the offensive, sweeping aside Shaidos' blade with a swing of his shield and thrusting, straight-armed, for his foeman's eyes.

He very nearly made it! Shaidos raised his target barely in time to save his eyes; even so, the hard-thrust weapon took him just under the rim of his gaudy helmet, sinking two inches into his forehead. Not realizing what had happened at first, Alexandros jerked with all his might to free his blade from whatever was locking it. Reluctantly, it came free with a sucking noise . . . and Shaidos' lifeless form pitched face-down on the sand at his feet.

That he bent to turn over Shaidos' body was all that saved Alexandros' life. The throwing-ax meant for his face caromed off his helmet, filling his head with flashing light and a red-black roar, and driving him to his knees. He neither saw nor heard Hulios, who followed his ax with a leap over the barrier and dashed toward the dizzied Sea Lord, shrieking and sobbing, the ax's twin held over his head. The slender boy managed two strides before a pair of black-shafted arrows thumped into his heaving chest. Still, dead on his feet, he essayed throwing the ax, but it flew far wide, striking the hot sand at almost the same time as Hulios' fine-boned body.

7

———————•═•───────▶━───•═•———————

"I am reliably informed that you could have slain him long before the fact, Lord Alexandros. It is worth too much to our two realms for you to take such needless risks."

Aldora had returned the day after the duel and Mara had finally managed the time to devote an entire evening to her guest-hostage.

Smiling into her eyes, he answered, "Viewing an action from afar and actually being in the heart of that action impart two very different perspectives, my lady. Many have informed me that I should have severed his knee tendons when I was behind him, just as many have chided me that I did not thrust below the edge of the backplate and skewer his kidney.

"I revere my lady and would not cause her distress, but I am a man and, as my lady must know, men fight." The voice was gentle, but emphatic.

Mara once more experienced that prickly tingling. *He* had spoken almost identical words, once.

"Lekos . . ." she began, without thinking.

The Sea Lord's easy smile returned to crinkle his young face. "Thank you, Mara. I'd far rather be considered your friend than a formal guest. And a first-name basis makes conversation infinitely easier."

Mara fought a quaver from her voice. "You are then called 'Lekos'?"

He shrugged. "My late father called me that; some of my older captains still do. But Mara, why stare you so oddly at me?"

She did not answer, but rather asked, "Lekos, how long have you been Sea Lord?"

"Five years, my la . . . Mara, since the death of my father."

"And your father reigned how long?"

"Almost twenty-five years, Mara."

"And it's been a good thirty years since any of your ships raided our coasts. Why? Aren't our people wealthy enough? Aren't our women sufficiently fair for the taste of your reavers?"

"So wealthy and fair, Mara, that my father was hard put to enforce his edict that this realm not be subject to raid. For a while it was touch and go, but as the older captains died or retired, he made it stick. Today, it is custom that High Lord Demetrios' coasts are sacrosanct."

"But," Mara pried, still far from satisfied, "Lord Pardos' men played merry hell on the coasts and rivers of Kehnooryos Ehlahs for two-score years, and his fathers before him. How came your father to order so radical a reversal of his ancestors' policies?"

Alexandros shook his head. "Mara, my father was not related to Lord Pardos by blood—not in direct lines of kinship, anyway. Pardos adopted him and compelled the Council of Captains to name him successor and support him. But years before he came to the Sea Isles, my father swore a lifelong oath of service to High Lord Demetrios. And my father was an honorable man. He kept to that oath all his life to the best of his ability, despite the fact that he served a cowardly swine."

Then, he related the story.

Lord Alexandros' tale

Prior to the fall of Kehnooryos Atheenahs and the subsequent establishment of the Confederation, Demetrios of Treeah-Pohtahmos had been sole and hereditary High Lord of Kehnooryos Ehlahs, which had since become the nucleus of the Confederation.

As Milo's tribe and their allies, the swelling army of the outlawed *Strahteegos*, Alexandros of Pahpahspolis, slowly moved eastward, unopposed, the High Lord found himself in an unenviable position, although his father had been a warrior-high-lord and had left him not only a well-filled treasury and thirty rich provinces ruled over by loyal nobles, but a large, tough, and formidable army.

Demetrios had been and could be and would be called many things in his seventy-odd years of life, but not, in the beginning, a militarist—that came later. His grasping, grafting, hedonistic clique replaced the administrators of his late father's honest and efficient civil service; within less than a year, Demetrios and his coterie had emptied the treasury.

Some of his army he frittered away in senseless wars that all ended in the loss of lands as well as men. The better condottas of Freefighters commenced to trickle away to seek the employ of lords who paid in hard coin rather than empty promises.

When he started to sell hard-won border provinces to foreigners to raise the cash to keep his sybaritic court supplied with necessary luxuries, the *Strahteegoee* and certain nobles who had been his father's closest friends and advisors decided that the young High Lord would destroy the realm, if not soon stopped. They carefully devised plans to topple their inept sovran and replace him with a council of military commanders until a new High Lord should be chosen.

Someone, nobody ever knew for certain whom, betrayed the projected coup to Demetrios, along with the names of nearly every man involved. The conspirators and their families —men, women, children, even babes-in-arms—were nearly all netted by the High Lord's men, although a few managed to flee into exile and some others fought their would-be captors to the death . . . these were the fortunate ones. The majority, regardless of age, sex, or known degree of involvement, were put to savage tortures. Many died under torture; many slew themselves to escape further torment. Demetrios saw that most suffered slow, degrading deaths, with their remains thrown into cesspools or the river. He kept some few maimed, broken men and women in his dungeons, having them occasionally brought up for the amusement of his depraved court.

When first the High Lord heard that nomads were coming

from the west he dispatched a good two-thirds of what army he had left. That army's gentle mission was to massacre the nomad warriors and take their women and children for sale as slaves. The nomads, warned by a deserter, trapped the army while it marched through a narrow mountain pass and virtually extirpated it.

The first of Demetrios' cities in their path, Theesispolis, fell to a sudden attack and most of its inhabitants were massacred. One of the High Lord's three remaining squadrons of Freefighters rode in pursuit of nomad raiders and had the misfortune to encounter a sizable war party; Demetrios had most of the survivors beheaded for having the effrontery to return alive.

That piece of barbarity, plus long-overdue wages, prompted the best of his two remaining squadrons to desert to the enemy. The Freefighters slew their Ehleenoee officers, took their arms, horses, and gear and rode out of the city after stopping long enough to loot a wing of the palace and to smash their way into the prison and free all prisoners who were in condition to travel.

Frantic with fear and lacking the money to hire more troops, he appealed to High Lord Hamos of Kehnooryos Makahdohnyah, who replied only with condolences and an offer of sanctuary. An appeal to Ohdessios, king of the fabulously wealthy Southern Kingdom, elicited a plea of poverty. When he appealed to his southern neighbor, King Zenos IX of Karaleenos, his messenger failed to return and Zenos' troops inaugurated a full-scale invasion of the southernmost provinces.

There was but one more source of possible aid, his distant kinsman, Pardos, Lord of the Sea Isles, and an infamous pirate. Since Demetrios had treated his navy as cavalierly as his land forces, he had to commandeer a merchant vessel to bear his messenger. The messenger returned with good tidings—or so he thought, since it was the first *positive* answer to the High Lord's desperate importunings. It seemed that while Lord Pardos was willing to discuss the rendering of aid to Kehnooryos Ehlahs in her extremity, he felt it proper that Demetrios, as supplicant, come to the court of the Sea Lord.

Demetrios raged! He screamed, swore, blasphemed, foamed,

and tore at his beard and hair. He slew three slaveboys and gravely injured a member of his court. He had the unfortunate messenger brutally tortured, emasculated, and blinded, then crucified with an iron pot filled with starving mice bound to his abdomen. He laid foul curses upon Pardos and all of his ancestors, gradually broadening his sphere of malediction to include the whole of the world and every living thing in it. Toward the end of his tantrum, he tore at his flesh with teeth and nails, slammed his head repeatedly against walls and columns, and rolled upon the floors, kicking his legs and sobbing like a spoiled, frustrated child.

Lastly, moaning piteously of the undeserved indignities being heaped upon him, he began to make grudging preparations for the voyage. He well knew—and so did everyone around him—that he had no option.

Lord Sergios, *Komees* of Pahpahspolis and High Admiral of the Navies of Kehnooryos Ehlahs, had never been upon the open ocean in all his young life; consequently, he was every bit as ill as Demetrios for most of the nearly two weeks that the wallowing merchantman took to reach the Sea Isles. The High Lord and the Admiral were the only nobles aboard, for it was a small ship and they, Demetrios' twenty bodyguards, and two slaveboys were all that could be accommodated.

At last, they were laid to, off the rocky, spray-shiny cliffs that were the northern side of the Sea Isles. Titos, sailing master and captain, had his crew put out a sea anchor, ran up signal flags, and then awaited the sign to proceed into the entry channel. They were allowed to wait for almost twenty-four hours before the clifftop fort puffed up a few blossoms of smoke. Then, propelled by slow strokes of the sweeps and depending for their very lives upon the leadsman straddling the bowsprit, Titos gingerly edged his ship into the narrow, treacherous channel.

Throughout the course of the long, halting passage, Demetrios fretted and cursed and fumed. He had been most loath to embark upon this abasement, but now that it was commenced, he wished to finish it quickly—like the fast swallowing of an unpleasant medicine.

Finally, the ship eased between the last of the jagged rocks and glided into the central lagoon, landlocked and placid, the water clear as blue-green glass and the bottom deceptively appearing but an arm's length from the viewer. The protrusions of dark rock were almost invisible, so covered were they by an endless profusion of fantastically colorful plant and animal life. Schools of tiny fish, scintillating as gemstones, darted to and fro and, a few hundred yards to port, a brace of flying fish broke the surface and sailed twice the length of the ship before reentering the water.

The ship's crew secured their sweeps and were making sail when Demetrios, his anger and frustration and even his sickness temporarily purged from him by the unquestionable beauty over which they were moving, rushed to the waist to hang over the rail. Fascinated by the marine panorama, he failed to notice the huge, dark shape just below the keel. Suddenly, a gigantic head broke the surface, immediately below him, and it seemed to his startled gaze that all the world had become a dark red gaping maw edged with huge conical white teeth.

Shrieking with terror, Demetrios thrust himself upward from off the rail with such force that he lost his footing and came down with a painful thump of soft bottom on hard deckboards.

From his seat, he screamed to the twenty black spearmen who were his bodyguards, "*Kill it!* Kill it! Do you hear us? We command you to kill the horrid, nasty thing! Kill it, now! At once!"

Two of the tall, slender men fitted short, broad-bladed darts to throwing sticks. One kicked off his slick-soled gilt sandals and climbed a few feet up the standing rigging. The other, who had been beside Lord Sergios on the small bridge, grasped a taut line and leaped onto the rail. But neither could spot a target; the monster had apparently departed as quickly and noiselessly as it had come.

Then, a long bowshot distant, a veritable forest of towering, black, triangular fins broke water and bore along on the same course as the ship.

"Sea serpents!" whimpered Demetrios. "They'll sink the ship and *eat* us!"

Endeavoring to not show his disgust, Titos shook his

grizzled head, saying, "Beggin' the High Lord's pardon, but them be grampuses, sorta half-porpoise an' half-whale. The lords of these isles hold converse with them creatures and, 'tis said they do his biddin'. I doubt me not that so many could go far toward the sinkin' of my ship, but . . ."

Before he could say more, the starboard side of the ship was struck twice, in rapid succession—a one-two that shook every line, beam, and timber of the vessel and rattled the teeth in men's heads. The aft spearman lost his footing on the polished rail and, stubbornly refusing to drop his spearstick and dart, hung by only his grip on the line, his sandaled feet frantically scrabbling for purchase on the smooth surfaces of the strakes.

Ere any could leap to the dangling man's assistance, a shadowy shape appeared beneath him. Again a head such as had frightened Demetrios rose above the water and a gaping mouth opened. While the spearman screamed, his legs and pelvis disappeared into that mouth and thick, two-inch teeth sank into the dark flesh . . . and then the fingers were gone from the line. Horrified, the crew and passengers could not but watch through the terrible clarity of the water as two streamlined black-and-white shapes, each above thirty feet long, worried the thrashing man apart, releasing a pink cloud of diluted blood. Voraciously, the monsters cleaned up the scraps, leaving but little to be picked at by the gleaming little fish.

On the heels of the gruesome episode, the ashy-faced High Lord fled to his cabin, leaving the deck to the crew, the nineteen sober and silent bodyguards, and Lord Sergios. During the couple of hours it took them to sail within sight of the main island, Kehnooryos Knossos, Titos and Lord Sergios lounged on the minuscule bridge and chatted. Every so often, whenever the array of six-foot fins changed directions, Titos shouted the change of course to the steersman. Between those times, however, he was able to ascertain that "Admiral" Sergios' intelligence was far greater than his foppish exterior promised, although his hands gave proof that he was no true seaman; nonetheless, he proved to know quite a bit of theoretical navigation.

Just before they entered the harbor mouth, a grampus sped past them and disappeared into the murky water of the harbor.

"Going to report to his master," remarked Titos.

Sergios nodded. "Many might call it sorcery, but I have heard that those who dwelt on the mainland, prior to the Punishment of God, domesticated all manner of unusual creatures—porpoises and seals among them."

"Aye," affirmed Titos. "I, too, have heard those tales. It is said that, even today, in the Witch Kingdom amid the Great Southern Swamp, full many a strange beast does the bidding of man."

At the mention of that unholy domain, Lord Sergios shuddered and hurriedly crossed himself.

"Why, strike me blind!" exclaimed Titos. "It has been years since I have seen any of your Lordship's class do that. I had thought me that the High Lord's new religion had completely supplanted the Ancient Faith—amongst the nobility of the capital, at least."

Sergios flushed and glanced about uneasily. "So it has, good Master Titos. The High Lord's orders notwithstanding, it is difficult to throw off the training of one's childhood and youth."

Now it was Titos who covertly eyed the deck and took care to see that his words would not be overheard. "Do you ever hear from your noble father, Lord Sergios? I served him, years agone, ere I went to sea. I still love him, despite what is said of him."

Sergios took Titos' arm and hustled him over to the rail. "Let none other hear you so avow, Master Titos," he whispered. "Else, some gray dawn will find you adorning a cross or immured in that place of horrors beneath the High Lord's prison, screaming for death.

"But in answer, no. Whether it's because he does not wish to endanger me, does not trust me, or has died, I do not know. I've not had one word from him since his flight."

"My Lord," hissed Titos fervently, "there are many who, like me, honor the memory of your noble father and what he tried to do for Kehnooryos Ehlahs . . ."

But he never finished, for it was then that Demetrios, closely guarded by his spearmen, waddled back on deck.

He was resplendent, hoping his sartorial elegance might possibly overawe the dread Lord Pardos and assure him the respect that the nasty pirate had thus far withheld. His sandals were not only gilded but adorned with small gems; so, too, were his gilded-suede "greaves." His kilt was of starched, snowy linen, and his cloth-of-gold "cuirass" had been stiffened with strips of whalebone. Rings flashed from every finger, almost matching the jewel-blaze that was the hilt and guard of his dress-sword. His flowing locks had been teased into ringlets, and hair, mustache and forked beard all shone and reeked of strongly perfumed oil.

Protocol in visits such as this really called for a military helmet, but the wearing of any kind of armor was unbearable to Demetrios. Metal was hot, binding, heavy, and terribly uncomfortable, and even leather caused one to perspire so. Therefore, his only head covering consisted of a narrow, golden circlet, surmounted by a frame of stiff wires. Over this was stretched another piece of cloth-of-gold that had been thickly sewn with seed pearls and was crested by a blue ostrich plume.

A massy gold chain hung between the two golden brooches that secured his cape of blue brocade. On the outer surface of the cape the Trident that was the badge of his house had been worked in silver wire. Broad golden bands adorned his smooth, pudgy, depilated forearms.

The pre-pubescent slaveboy who was to accompany him was attired similarly, in addition to being heavily cosmetized. His guard was to consist of an even dozen of his black spearmen, officered by Lord Admiral Sergios. The other seven spearmen he ordered to guard his cabin and protect his possessions from wandering pirates or thieving crewmen.

Followed by his cortege, the High Lord of Kehnooryos Ehlahs proceeded to an awning-covered section of the waist and awaited the arrival of a litter or chariot to convey him. Two hours later, as the sun was sinking behind the western cliffs, and the mosquitoes were venturing out for the night's feasting, the High Lord of Kehnooryos Ehlahs and his retinue were still waiting.

The blacks were relaxed, patient; Lord Sergios kept glancing warily at his unpredictable lord; Demetrios was nearing a state of murderous anger. Such discourtesy from a fellow-noble-Ehleen could just not be tolerated! All at once, he half turned, jerked the slaveboy closer, and slammed the back of his heavy hand across the child's face. Then he felt a little better.

Almost instantly, the little minion's nose began to bleed and Demetrios sent him below to change clothing with the other minion, promising the terrified child dire punishment if his blood should damage the costly stuffs in which he was attired.

While the little slaves did his bidding, the High Lord ordered Titos to fetch one of the dockside idlers who had been splicing ropes, mending nets, and chatting while gawking at the newcomers. The captain shortly returned with an ageless, weather-browned man and Demetrios commanded Sergios to question the oldster.

Shuffling his big, tar-stained feet on the worn stones of the quay, the man heard Sergios out, then replied nonchalantly in atrociously accented Ehleenokos. "Oh, aye, Cap'n, Ol' Shortnose kens you're here, right enough. For a chariot, you'll have a long walk, 'cause it ain't no horses on these here islands. Ain't no need for the critters, nor no graze, neither—the sheeps and goats and pigs gits it all.

"As for a litter . . ." Before continuing, he ran a tarry forefinger far up one nostril, withdrew it, and critically examined his findings, then casually wiped them on the seat of his filthy cotton breeches. "Wal, last litter I recollect seein' was made outa two boat hooks and a slicker—or was it a boat cloak?—and they used it to carry what was left of ol' Zohab up to the priest's place, the day that there big shark got inta the l'goon and chawed off his laigs, 'fore the Orks drove it off'n him. He died, o'course. Wouldn'ta wanted to live, no how, 'cause the bugger'd torn off his parts, too.

"*Manalive!* He'uz some kinda big shark. You awta seed him. The Orks run him inta shaller water and we harpooned him and drug him up on the rocks and clubbed him 'til he stopped floppin', then took a broad ax and took off his bottom jaw. 'Cause, you know, his kind'll bite even after they dead. Forty foot long, he were, and weighed nigh on to eight thousan' pound, after he'z cut up. Never see'd a shark like him, I hadn', and I hopes I never see another'n. He'uz a kinda dirty-white and he wan't shaped like most sharks, more like a tunny, I'd say.

"Well, didn' nobody wanta eat none of him, and I can't say I blames 'em none, what with him a-eatin' the bes' parta ol' Zohab, like he done. His tooths, the mosta 'em was too big for arrow points, so we give 'em to ol' Foros, the dart-maker, and you know what he tolt me?"

"Shut up!" screamed Demetrios, his face empurpled. "You garrulous old fool, we don't want to hear another word about sharks. All we wish to be told is when Lord Pardos intends to send an honor guard to convey or conduct us to his palace."

The Sea Islander gave his crotch a good scratching, then answered: "Well, cain't say as how I knows what a honor guard's like, but you cain't miss Ol' Short-Nose's place, seein' it's the onlies' place on this here islan's got more'n two stories. And it's right on top the hill, too, and that's good, 'cause the muskeetas don't offen get thet far. And you jes' wouldn' b'lieve how bad they gets sometimes. Course, they don't bother dark-skinned folks like me near as much as they do the pore bugger's got lighter skin.

"And, you know, you can b'lieve me or not, but it's exac'ly the same way with fleas, too! Unless he's a-starvin' to death, a flea'll pass right over a dozen fellers got dark skin and chomp right down on a light-skinned feller evertime. Thet's why I tells these here light 'uns thet the bestes' thang they c'n do is to git theyselfs jest as dark as they can as quick as they can.

"I tell you, I don' know where they all comes from—muskeetas, I mean—but they jes' lays up all day a-honin' their boardin' pikes. And come sundown they blows the conch and theys out a-reavin, ever' mother's son of em. Course, the fleas and the lice is at it day *and* night, you know. But the lice ain't so bad—they only gits in your hair. Course, that's bad iffen you got a lotta hair, like you young fellers do. But iffen you like me . . ." He broke off, staring at the High Lord.

Demetrios' face had passed from lividity to absolute pallor. So angry was he that he was unable to do more than splutter and beat his clenched fists on the ship's rail. His features were jerking uncontrollably and a vein in his forehead throbbed violently.

Finally, he managed to gasp, "The gods damn your guts, you putrid, wormy, old swine! You tell us what we want to know, or you'll be drinking a broth of your eyes and your clacking tongue!"

The brown-skinned man regarded Demetrios without fear, then noisily hawked and spat on the dock. "I'm a-answerin you the bes' I knows how. I don' know if you can git away with talkin' to folks like you jes' talked to me where you come from, but Ol' Short-Nose's rules is thet name an' threat callin' is reasons enough to call a feller to stan' an' fight, man to man, iffen you're a mind to.

"Now your ship-master asted me to come over to here and I dropped my work and come right on over. Didn' I? I done tried to be perlite an' helpful, cause I could see you was a stranger an' a landlubber, to boot. An' I's took me a pure lot offen you, cause you's a furriner and I figgered me mebbe they don't teach folks decent manners where you come from. You may be a big mucketymuck in your parts, but you ain't in 'em now, lordy-boy.

"I be a ol' man now. But, in my day, I shipped with Ol' Short-Nose an' with Rockhead, his pa, an' with Red-Arm, his uncle, too. An' it's many a good man's guts I done spilled— in fac', thet's whut they still calls me, Gutcutter Yahkohbz. Nowadays, I don't even own me a sword, got no use for one no more; but I do have me a good knife, yet." He shifted a wide, heavy-bladed dirk around to his right side, where its worn hilt was clearly visible.

"Now, I may be three times as ol' as you, lordy-boy, at leas' twicet it, an' you got you a sword, too. But I'd still lay you a helmet fulla gold to a pot fulla piss thet if I'uz to stan' for my rights, you'd be a snack for the Orks in 'bout one minute. But I ain't gonna do it, sonny, so it ain't no call for you to wet your pants a worryin'.

"I ain't, 'cause I can take me one look at you an' tell it wouldn' be no' fight nor no fun. B'sides, I got me more important thangs to git done, 'fore the lasta the daylight's gone."

With that, he spun on his heel and limped back to the rope

he had been splicing, casting not another glance at the High
Lord of Kehnooryos Ehlahs.

Between them, Lord Sergios and Master Titos managed to
persuade Demetrios not to order his blacks to spear the old
pirate, pointing out that, as the man was obviously free, such
might be considered murder hereabouts, and the cashless
High Lord called upon to pay a blood price. Far better, they
argued, to discuss the incident at a propitious time with Lord
Pardos, leaving punishment for the old man's unpardonable
crimes to his own sovran.

The sprawling, three-story residence of Lord Pardos occu-
pied most of an artificial mesa and was built mostly of the
dark native stone. For many long minutes after arriving on
the hilltop, Demetrios had to lean, gasping and shuddering,
his red face streaming sweat, against the wall near the entrance. None of the black spearmen, nor Lord Sergios, nor
even the little slave, was in the least winded, but it had been
years since the High Lord had been forced to *walk* up an entire half mile of hillside.

Within an outer court, lamps and torches flared an orange
glow above the wall, while the mingled sounds of bellowing
laughter, shouts, feminine squeals, and snatches of wild, barbaric music smote on Demetrios' ears, and his nose registered
the smells of roasted meat and wine.

Outside the high, double-valved gate hung a scarred brass
gong. When Demetrios had recovered sufficiently to stand
erect, Lord Sergios drew his sword and pounded on the gong.
Abruptly, most of the noise from within subsided. Then one
of the portals was swung half open and they were confronted
by a gap-toothed, one-eyed giant of a man, wearing a well-
oiled tunic of loricated armor and a brass-and-leather helm,
with a huge, spiked ax on his shoulder.

"Well?" he snarled. "State your business, an' it better be
good!"

Sergios sheathed his blade, cleared his throat, and spoke
formally: "Sir, please announce to your Lord that Demetrios,
High Lord of Kehnooryos Ehlahs, requests audience with his
cousin, Pardos, Lord of the Sea Isles."

The mammoth pirate squinted his eye and demanded, "An'
be you him?"

The High Lord roughly shoved Sergios aside and took what he hoped was an arrogant stance in front of this smelly, frightening man. "*We* are Demetrios, my man!" He tried to say the words firmly and deeply, but as he was still a bit out of breath, what came from his lips was a piping falsetto.

The squinted eye widened. "*You* be the cousin of Ol' Short-Nose? Well, I'll be damned!" remarked the warrior. Then he slammed the gate in Demetrios' face.

When the gate was reopened, the axman was backed up by a half dozen well-armed men, two of them blacks of very similar build and features to the High Lord's guards.

"*You*," the one-eyed man said, pointing a dirty finger at Demetrios, "can come in, you and your boy. And your guard-captain, too." He indicated Lord Sergios, who was wearing a real cuirass and helmet in addition to his sword and ornate dagger. "First your guard-captain has to be disarmed and searched for hidden weapons. The resta your guards gotta stay here."

He spun about, then growled over his shoulder. "Now, come on. Ol' Short-Nose don't much care for waitin'."

The High Lord's gaze had never before rested on so villainous a throng as the fifty-odd men who sat on benches or sprawled on cushions the length of the courtvard. Few seemed to possess more than a trace of Ehleen blood, most were obviously barbarians, and barbaric in taste as well as in lineage. Priceless jewelry adorned greasy tatters of once fine clothing or canvas jerkins; plain and well-worn sword hilts jutted from ornate scabbards. Ears and noses had been pierced to receive golden hoops or jeweled studs. Many were clad only in short trousers and, on their hairy skins, savage tattoos writhed around and across networks of white or pink or purple scars. Some were missing a part of an arm or a hand or fingers, many lacked front teeth, all or parts of ears, and one had replaced a missing eye with a huge opal. Another had painted the multitudinous scars on his chest, joining them with lines of color so as to spell out obscene words and phrases in Ehleenokos.

Though the laughter of the men was loud and frequent, the faces of one and all were hard—hard as the muscles under their dirty, sweaty hides. The high walls stopped most of the cooling breezes and the courtyard had to be smelled to be believed. Alone, the mingled odors—of fish and cooked flesh and wine and ale, of cooking oil and lamp fat and wood smoke, of unwashed bodies and sweat—would have been more than sufficient to turn Demetrios' stomach; but there was more, and it was, by his lights, even more sickening.

Where, at Demetrios' parties, each guest was provided with a pretty, little slaveboy, these uncultured primitives actually had *women* at their sides or sprawled across them! And most of the vile creatures were less than half clad, while some were completely nude. To the High Lord it was painfully obvious that none in this court was in any sense of the word civilized, for what civilized man could force himself to eat and drink while within proximity of so many utterly disgusting creatures?

Advancing up the cleared space between the revelers, he was fighting to hold down his gorge when, ere he could be aware of her intentions, a brown-haired strumpet flung both her arms about his neck and kissed him full on his mouth.

It was the final straw! Demetrios frantically fought his way out of the laughing woman's noisome embrace, pushing her with such force that she measured her length upon the floor tiles. For a moment he just stood, stock-still, his face a greenish white. Then it came—doubling over, he spewed out the contents of his stomach.

All the confusion stilled to a deathly silence, broken only by the tortured gagging of the vomiting man. Then one of three men seated behind a scarred table at the end of the courtyard slammed the palm of a four-fingered hand onto the wine-wet table and, lolling back in his chair, began to roar and snort with laughter. His two companions joined in, as did some of the other men and women. A few cracked ribald jests at the wretched High Lord's condition, but most simply chuckled briefly, then went back to the business of the evening—eating and drinking and kissing and fondling.

He retched in agony until, at last, his heaving stomach became convinced further efforts would yield no further results. As he straightened—gasping, livid, his bloodshot eyes streaming tears—the little minion snatched a nameless piece of

clothing from off a nearby stool and began to dab at the wet
stains on the High Lord's attire.

Demetrios felt well served. Here was an object on which
he could safely vent the anger provoked by his embarrass-
ment and frustration. His foot lashed out viciously; it caught
the hapless child in the ribs, propelling him six feet to crash
into a full wine barrel. As the stunned slaveboy crumpled,
one of the women rushed to kneel beside him and took his
bloody little head into her lap. Dipping a piece torn from her
sheer skirt into the top of the barrel, she commenced to wipe
the child's forehead and cheeks.

Despite an unsteadiness in his legs, Demetrios—horrified
that one of his favorite minions should be defiled by the
touch of a *woman*—started toward her, hissing, "You putrid,
stinking bitch, you, get your hands off him this instant! Do
you hear me, shameless she-thing?"

The woman appraised him briefly, sneered, then turned
back to the boy. Infuriated, the High Lord advanced until he
stood over her, raised one be-ringed, fat-fingered hand to
strike her . . . and was suddenly frozen by the coldest,
hardest voice he had ever in his life heard.

"Touch her, you mincing pig, and you'll lose every finger
on that hand, one joint per hour!"

The speaker was seated on a low couch beside a tall, red-
haired woman. He wore finely tooled knee boots, loose
trousers cinched with a wide belt, and a cotton-lawn shirt
open to the waist. A slender dagger was thrust into his belt,
but he was otherwise unarmed amongst the weapons-bristling
throng.

However, when Demetrios got a good look at the speaker's
face, he could have again been ill. A wide scar ran from high
on the left temple and on down to the chin, barely missing
the eye; the tip of the man's nose was gone and so was half
the right ear; but most hideous of all, at some time an inch-
wide hole had been gouged or cut into the man's right cheek
and, in healing, had never closed and yet his eyes and hair
and bone structure led the High Lord to think that this man
could be a *Kath'ahróhs*—a pureblood Ehleen.

With considerable effort, Demetrios partially overcame his

fear and repugnance. "How . . . *dare* you so address us! Do you know who we are?"

Even the chuckle was hard and cold. "Fat as you are, I can see why you employ the plural when referring to yourself. Yes, I know *who* you are, as well as *what* you are . . . and it sickens me to have to acknowledge any degree of kinship to a thing like you, *cousin.*

"As for me, I am Pardos, Lord of the Sea Isles. You are here to beg me for help. Seeing you, I can now understand why you need help. If you are a fair sample of what the Ehleenoee nobility of the mainland are become, may God help us. If all are such as you, *cousin*—a peacock-pretty pederast with a voice like a girl and no more body hair than the boy-children you beat and abuse, with less courage than a baby mouse—then mayhap a mainland ruled by clean, normal, courageous, and uncomplicated barbarians would make for better neighbors."

Arising, the Sea Lord strode over to his "guest," then strolled slowly around him, critically eyeing his baubles and attire. Suddenly, he snatched out the High Lord's sword and examined the stones of the golden hilt and guard; at length, and without apparent strain, he snapped off the two feet of dull blade and tossed the hilt to the red-haired woman.

"The High Lord's guest-gift to you, Kahndees."

She fingered the showy treasure—which was worth fully as much as Titos' ship—and then her full lips curved in a mocking smile and she spoke in Ehleenokos as pure as Demetrios' own. "I cannot truly express my thanks, My Lord Demetrios." A hint of laughter lurked in her well-modulated voice.

Pardos flicked the tip of the broken blade at the stiffened pleats of Demetrios' linen kilt. "A skirt suits you well, *cousin.* Generally, your kind *are* more woman than man."

The High Lord quavered: "It . . . the kilt . . . is the ancient garb . . . of the Ehleen warrior."

"You?" Pardos snorted. "A warrior?" Then, tapping the blade on the cloth-of-gold breastplate, he added, "This is supposed to be a cuirass, I take it; why, it'd not turn a well-thrown pebble. As for your helmet . . ." He jabbed the silver-washed skewer through the stiffened cloth and snapped

the entire contrivance up off Demetrios' head, then flipped it to the red-haired woman.

"Payment for your kiss, Mahndah. Our guest is generous."

She placed the *chapeau* on her brown curls, then made a deep obeisance. "My deepest thanks, Lord Demetrios, I'll wear it in memory of you."

Sweat streamed down the High Lord's jowls. He was now certain that this horrible monster intended to kill him when he had finished toying with him.

"Tch-tch," clicked Pardos, noticing the copious perspiration. "You are unaccustomed to our climate here, *cousin*. You will be much cooler if you'll but remove that heavy cape. Here . . . let me do it for you; after all, you are my guest."

After unpinning the brooches, he disconnected one end of the gold chain and slipped the cape from the High Lord's shaking shoulders. Snapping the pieces together again, he turned and tossed them to the woman who knelt by the wine barrel.

"This is for the lad, Tildah. But never fear, there'll be something pretty for you, ere long."

Taking the High Lord's soft white hand, Pardos commenced to pull at the showiest ring, an emerald-cut diamond set in reddish gold.

Demetrios vainly tried to jerk his hand free of the crushing grip. *"No!"* he whimpered. "No, please, no. Oh, what have I done to you that you should so use me, my lord?"

The look that then came into Pardos' black eyes stung his captive far more than did the contemptuous slap dealt him. The Sea Lord's voice became glacial. "You are what you are, you gutless thing of indeterminate sex. But what is far worse is that I, God help me, am of the same blood as you; and you make it obvious that our blood is tainted."

He might have said more, had not a hand grasped his shoulder and spun him about. Sergios had had to surrender sword and dirk and cuirass to gain admittance to the courtyard, but when he saw his sovran struck, mere lack of weapons could not hold him back. When he confronted the pirate, the eyes that glared from beneath his helmet's rim were every bit as hard as Pardos' own.

"Dog and son of a dog!" he hissed in a low voice. "Has your house sunk so low that you forget who and what you are? We three are Ehleenoee—*Kath'ahróhs* nobles. As such we do not degrade ourselves, *or one another,* before barbarians!"

Pardos looked honestly amazed at the interruption. But he snapped, "And who are you, my young cockerel, to instruct me in the manners of nobility?"

Sergios bowed stiffly, though his eyes never left those of Lord Pardos. "Lord Sergios, Admiral of Kehnooryos Ehlahs, my lord."

Pardos nodded and his frown softened a little. "A fellow seaman, eh? And if my eyes don't deceive me, a *real* man, as well. If you're not this thing's kind, why would you defend him?"

Sergios heaved a deep sigh. "Because I must be true to my word, my lord. High Lord Demetrios is my sovran and, long ago, I swore to serve and protect him. Protect him, I will, my lord, to the last drop of my blood."

Without warning, Pardos' muscular arm shot out to the side. All he said was "Sword." A short, heavy one was slapped into his waiting palm.

"Words lack intrinsic value without deeds to back them, Admiral Sergios," said Pardos, stepping to the clear area before the large table and scuffing his boot soles on the tiles, the sword held casually at low guard. "Let us see some of that blood you've pledged this hunk of rotten offal."

Instinctively, Sergios' hand went to his scabbard, but came away empty. "My lord, my weapons are at your gate and . . ."

Pardos sneered. "To the last drop of your blood, eh? When you knew yourself to be unarmed and thought that fact would save you. *Fagh!* You're as bad as your mistress, here." He waved contemptuously at Demetrios.

Sergios flushed and shook his head vigorously. "Your pardon, my lord, but you misunderstand. If your men will return my sword or loan me a weapon, even a dagger, I shall be at your pleasure."

"You're at my pleasure, anyway, mainlander," barked Pardos shortly. "As you are, you saw fit to insult me; as you are, you will fight me, by God. You get no weapons from *my* men!"

The expression on Sergios' handsome face never altered. He bowed his head slightly while his quick mind assessed his chances, finding them slim, indeed. His leather gambeson might turn a glancing blow and its knee-length skirt with its scales of silver-washed steel would hopefully protect his loins and thighs. His helm, though highly decorated, was honest steel, but his armbands were but brass. Surreptitiously, he glanced about, then quickly crouched and both arms shot out, one to grasp the broken blade of Demetrios' sword, the other to jerk the heavy cape from the loose grip of the woman by the barrel.

Rapidly, he whirled the cape tightly around his left hand and forearm. Then he assumed a knife-fighter's stance, his knees slightly flexed, his left foot forward, his edgeless strip of steel at his right thigh.

"I told you, you young cur," shouted Pardos, "that you were to have no weapons! Drop the blade and the cape . . . *now!*"

Sergios gave a tight smile. "I suggest that my lord see now if *his* deeds can give value to *his* words. You'll take these poor weapons only from my corpse, you know." Then his smile became mocking. "Or does my lord fear to face an *armed* man, eh? Take time for a cup of strong wine, my lord. Some say that it imparts courage. . . ."

No serpent ever struck as quickly as did Pardos. Sergios managed to deflect most of the slash with his improvised shield and the flimsy armlet beneath it. Even so, the pirate's blade drew blood. But even as he took the wound, Sergios rushed inside Pardos' guard and the lights glinted on the blur of silvered-steel with which he lunged at the bare chest before him.

At the last split second, Pardos leaped backward and parried the thrust, meaning to beat Sergios' blade upward. But the first contact of sword to the inferior steel shattered poor Sergios' inadequate armament like glass.

Stamping and roaring, Pardos swung at the angle of Sergio's neck and shoulder. The younger man's duck saved his life. The sword struck the helmet, instead, denting the thick steel and sending it spinning through the air. The force of the blow hurled Sergios to the ground. Pardos hacked at his downed opponent again and again, but Sergios rolled from beneath the blows. Finally, he regained his footing and shrewdly kicked Pardos' right wrist—already somewhat weakened by the repeated impacts of sword on stone. The pirate sword went clattering down the length of the courtyard.

"Now, my lord," Sergios said, grinning, wiping the back of his right hand across his brow, trying to keep the blood from his split scalp out of his eyes, "we two are a bit closer to evenly matched."

Pardos drew his dagger and slowly advanced. Sergios tried to bring up his left arm, but it hung limp and dripping; the slashed cape was now wet and heavy. With a snarl, Pardos leaped onto the weakened man and, even as they crashed to the tiles, he secured Sergios' right wrist. Then he pressed the needle point of his dagger into the younger man's throat. Blood welled up around the bluish steel.

But he stayed his hand, saying, "You never had the ghost of a chance, Lord Admiral Sergios, and I think you knew it, yet you fought . . . and fought damned well. If you'll but admit that you lied in naming me dog, then plead for your life—I'll spare you."

As much as the hard-pressed steel would allow it, Sergios shook his bloody head. "Thank you, my lord, but I must refuse. Men of my House do not lie, nor do they beg."

"*Nonononol*" shrieked Demetrios, palms flat on his ashen cheeks. "He . . . he really means it, Sergios! He'll kill you . . . and then, probably *me*, too! I . . . I *command* you, tell him you lied, beg him for your life!"

Sergios' gaze shifted to the High Lord and his look was pitying. "Lord Demetrios, I am your sworn man, this you well know. I have forsaken friends and . . . and even my loved family in your service. Many of your commands have been distasteful; nonetheless, they *were* your commands and, God help me, I discharged my orders. But, my lord, only my body is sworn to you . . . not my soul, my honor."

Such was his pique at the words that Demetrios forgot everything—time, place . . . and circumstances, as well. He stamped his foot. "*Pagh!* Now you're talking like that treach-

erous old fool of a father you had. We'd credited you as a
civilized man, a man of intelligence, a realist. Without life,
you fool, honor has no value, if it has any, anyway . . .
which we doubt."

Sergios' look of pity intensified and his voice, too, became
pitying. "Poor my lord. In this, as in so many things, your
mind has become twisted. To you, realism is cynicism; intelligence denotes but the word for a constant agreement with
you; civilized is your term for a life devoted entirely to de-
bauchery, senseless cruelty, and perversion.

"To you, honor does not have value, for you lack any
shred of it and, truly, you know not its meaning. My lord,
your poor, sick mind has reversed the order of things; without honor, life has no value. To die here and now, with
honor, under this brave lord's blade, will be a quick and almost painless death. To live, with dishonor as you command
me, would be death, too, but a slow and unbearable death."

His eyes locked again with Pardos' and he smiled. "I am
ready, my lord. You are a far better man than the lord I
served. It will be an honor to die under your hand. Let your
stroke be hard and true."

"It will be both, Lord Sergios," replied Pardos. "I derive no
joy from the sufferings of *brave* men. You are truly a man of
honor and all men should give credit to your house. Please,
tell me its name, that I and my men may remember it and
you in times to come."

"I have the honor to be the son of Alexandros of
Pahpahspolis, formerly *Strahteegohs* of Strahteegohee of
Kehnooryos Ehlahs."

Lord Pardos' voice held a gravity bordering upon awe.
"Your father was a man of far nobler and purer lineage than
those he served. And I had heard that his son still served
Basil's son. When I learned *what* you are, I should have
known *who* you are, Lord Sergios.

"It is said that blood will tell. Your's certainly has, and I'll
not bear the guilt of shedding more of the precious stuff. To
butcher an unnatural swine is one thing; to murder a valiant
man of high and ancient nobility is quite another."

He withdrew his dagger and stood up. Sergios, too, tried to
rise, but fell back, groaning between clenched teeth. With

hard face, Pardos strode purposefully toward Demetrios. At the sight of that bloody dagger's approach, the High Lord's bladder and knees failed him at the same time. Groveling in a spreading pool of his urine, he clasped his be-ringed hands and raised them beseechingly.

"Oh, please . . . *please!*" he blubbered. "*Please* don't kill me . . . we . . . I . . . you . . . you can have everything, *everything!* Here!" Frantically, he stripped off all the rest of his rings, fumbled them into one cupped palm, and extended them in Pardos' direction.

Coldly furious, the Sea Lord slapped the proferred hand, sending the costly baubles flying in all directions, and started to recommence his advance on his victim, only to find that some weight was impeding his leg. He looked down to find that Sergios' unwounded right arm was wrapped about his booted ankle.

A wide pool of blood marked the place where the young admiral had lain. And a broad, red trail showed the path along which he had dragged himself. Now that he had turned onto his belly, the jagged rent that one of Pardos' blows had torn in the gambeson diagonally down from the left shoulder was very obvious. Through this dangerous wound, as well as those in his left arm and his scalp, his life was gradually oozing out. The only color left on his face were the streaks of gore from his head and from the place his teeth had met in his lower lip.

But his eyes burned feverishly and his grip on Pardos' leg, though weak, was dogged. And his voice, when he spoke, was surprisingly firm.

"You'll not slay him . . . my lord—not while yet I live."

"I promised to spare *your* life, noble Sergios," Pardos answered gently, "not the life of this thing."

Sergios coughed and a shower of pink froth sprayed from his mouth. His voice weakened perceptibly. "My . . . life . . . pledged to . . . him. Cannot live in . . . honor . . . not pro . . . protect him."

"Brother." Though urgent, Pardos' voice was infinitely tender. "Your efforts are *killing* you. This man-shaped thing is not worth a life, especially a life such as yours."

"Lord Demetrios," Sergios said, gasping, "far worse . . . you know. Still . . . *my* lord."

Pardos flung the dagger in the path of his sword. Spinning, he knelt and gently disengaged Sergios' arm from his ankle.

"Noble Sergios, your courage has purchased two lives this night. Much as I want his death, the life of so rare a man as you is too high a price."

Raising his head, the Sea Lord bellowed, "Zaileegh, Eegohr, Benáhree, Kohkeenoh-Djahn, to me!"

With the aid of the four captains, Pardos had the fainting Sergios lifted and laid face-down on the hastily cleared large table. Under the directions of the red-haired Kahndees, a trio of women set about removing his gambeson, while two others bared his left arm and applied a tourniquet, and still another sponged his face with undiluted wine.

Brusquely, Pardos issued orders.

"Zaileegh, fetch me Master Gahmahl and his assistants. Tell him the nature of the injuries, that he may know what to bring. And emphasize that this man means much to me. And . . . , just in case, you'd better bring Father Vokos, too."

"Kohkeenoh-Djahn, collect your crew and ready your ship. You sail at dawn to convey High Lord Demetrios back to his sty, along with any of his who wish to return. I promised I'd let him live, and live he will—but not here. Let him pollute some other realm. His ship and all she carries are mine; have it seen to. Bring his slaves to me and see how many of his ship's crew you can recruit. Have Ngohnah talk to his bodyguard; spearmen like them are hard to find."

"Benáhree, have our fat guest stripped of the warrior's garb his flesh profanes. Find him some women's clothing. Then lodge Princess Perversia somewhere for the night . . . bearing in mind her predilection for dung, of course."

"Eegohr, with the good Father on the way, we'd better see about getting clothing on our ladies."

The High Lord, clad in an old, torn shift, spent the remainder of the night in six inches of slime at the bottom of a recently abandoned cesspool. Before dawn he was dragged from his noisome prison and chivvied down to the harbor. There, with much rough horseplay, Zaileegh's crew stripped him and hosed him down, dragged him aboard *The Golden Dream*, and threw him into a dank rope locker, where he was shortly joined by Captain Titos.

In addition to her three sails, Captain Zaileegh's ship mounted two banks of long sweeps on either board and, with a crew of over one hundred fifty, made good time—in wind or calm, twenty-four hours a day. Unlike Titos' merchant-vessel, *The Golden Dream* had been built for speed and ease of handling. Furthermore, both of her masts could be un-stepped and laid out to lessen wind resistance when she was being propelled by oar power. All these factors contributed to the fact that she reached the coastal swamps of Kehnooryos Ehlahs in only six days.

Captain Zaileegh moored in a creek mouth until sundown. Then the ship was rowed up the wide, sluggish Blue River, reaching the all but deserted docks of Kehnooryos Atheenahs well before dawn. Their two passengers, securely bound and gagged, were dumped on the largest dock. Then the pirates beat their way back downriver.

8

Refilling her goblet and Alexandros', Mara nodded, "When first Milo and I came here, there were rumors that Demetrios had tried to flee by sea, but that he had met with some misfortune and returned. He only discussed the episode if he was given no choice; even then he seldom told the same stories twice. Now I can understand why. Of course, he was then unaware that he was one of us, the Undying; he has become far more courageous since then.

"So you, Lekos, are the grandson of that other Lekos. But what of your father, Sergios? How did he come to remain amongst the pi . . . people of the Sea Islands?"

"Well, Mara, my father's wounds were grave—he nearly died of them. His recuperation required many months, and during those months Lord Pardos and his wife came to add love to the respect they bore him. So, when once more he was able to walk and join his host at table, Pardos and Kahndees set about persuading him to stay. Nor was it difficult. When he heard that his father was dead, slain by Demetrios in a duel . . ."

Mara shook her head. "It did not happen precisely in that way, but continue, Lekos."

"With my grandfather, the man who had extracted my father's oath to devote his life to Basil's son, dead by the hand of Basil's son, Lord Pardos and Father Vokos—who knew more regarding the ancient customs and manners of the Ehleenoee than any man I have ever met—were able to convince my father that he was at last freed of his vow."

"It is true," agreed Mara. "According to the old forms, the demise of the recipient of an oath frees him who made it of all obligation."

"But," added Alexandros, "my father never felt free of *all* obligation, else I would not now be in your palace, Mara.

"When once more he could swing a sword and do spear-work and the wearing of armor failed to tire him, he grew restless and badgered Pardos until it was finally agreed that he might begin to earn his keep.

"Mara, there are many of your mainlanders who say that we of the Sea Isles are barbarians. It is true, but only in the sense that precious few of us have much Ehleen blood, and most of that is highly diluted. And at the time of which I am speaking, Lord Pardos and my father were the only *Kath'ahróhs* in the realm.

"Mara, our name for all who are not Sea Islanders is *Pseheesteesohee*—liars, in Merikanos. Our people never lie, not to each other, nor do they steal from other Sea Islanders— not because of any fearsome punishment, but because either would be dishonorable. We are, needs must, a tightly knit and strongly interdependent society, and newcomers either learn to be honorable or they do not long survive.

"Our only hereditary title is that of Sea Lord, and even a legitimate heir may be set aside should the Council of Captains find serious fault in him. A Sea Lord inherits only ownership of the Sea Isles, the structures on the various islands, the shipyard, docks, and his predecessor's personal property. Captains may buy and sell ships—they own all of them—but everyone pays rent for their dwellings and storehouses to the Sea Lord, who also receives a small percentage of profitable voyages, exacts fees for the use of the shipyard and for harborage, and collects buyers' taxes on exports from the merchants who come to trade with us.

"Few of our men live long, Mara. Nine out of ten die before they are thirty. Because of this and because of the length of time a ship may be at sea, our women practice polyandry, and it has worked well over the years. Lord Pardos had suffered an injury in his youth that rendered him sterile, so he had my father wed Lady Kahndees. She bore him my two older half-brothers, but both were slain while I was yet a child.

"Father accompanied other captains on many voyages, distinguishing himself in many ways. He had been in the Sea Isles for five years when, at the death of Captain Kleev during a sea fight, Kleev's crew elected him their captain. He had made many friends, and when he brought Kleev's ship back in, the Council unanimously confirmed his captaincy.

"In only three years, father was a senior captain, owning and commanding nine ships, and raiding as far away as *Eespahneeah, Eerlahntheeah*, and even farther north. Two years before my birth, he sailed his ships into the tideless sea, from which our people came so long ago. While his ships scattered to raid, he visited *Pahlyohs Ehlahs*, where he was well and courteously received. He stayed three months, and when he sailed to rendezvous with his ships, he brought with him his bride, my noble mother.

"When I was a child of nine years, Lord Pardos sat feasting with his captains one night. All at once, he stood up with a look of agony on his face, then fell in a swoon. Master Saheed, who was then the principal surgeon, came just as Lord Pardos awakened to discover that he could not move his left arm or leg.

"It was shortly afterward that he had himself borne to the Council of Captains and, before them, formally adopted my father as his heir. Later, he exacted promises from the senior captains that they would all support my father and me after him. Six months later, Lord Pardos died and my father was acclaimed Sea Lord."

"And you became the same, upon your father's death," Mara added, finishing for him. "But your lady-mother, what of her?"

Alexandros grinned. "*Mothers*, Mara, don't forget my father had two wives and I honor them both. Mother Kahndees died one night in her sleep soon after father died. Mother Ahnah is now wed to Senior Captain Yahnekos, whom you met."

"Only one husband?" smiled Mara mischievously. "Who comforts her while Yahnekos is out raiding?"

Alexandros chuckled. "She is only forty, Mara, and still a

handsome woman. I am certain that she wants not for 'companionship,' for it is not as here. Her lovers have naught to fear from Yahnekos."

Mara became serious. "You are, then, of a lusty people, Lekos. Yet, while you have been my guest, noble women have thrown themselves at you and you have been offered the usual slavegirl-bedwarmers. You have refused one and all. Tell me why . . . and don't give me the put-off that so charmed those sluts at Lady Ioanna's orgy, either."

His black eyes bored into hers. "But what I said, that night, was completely true, Mara," he said slowly. "There is but one woman in your court who stirs me, but . . . she is wed to a powerful lord. And your mainland customs differ from ours."

Mara steepled her fingers. "Not entirely, Lekos. The Ehleenoee's do, yes; but the Horseclanswomen have many freedoms, since most clans have always reckoned descent through the mother. In the settled life the tribe is now leading, their customs are undergoing slow changes, but clan matrons are still free to couple with the men of their choosing . . . so long as they do not overstep discretion and are careful of degrees of kinship."

She leaned forward, saying, "Lekos, Undying Goddess I may be to the tribe, but I am still a woman. And I will admit that I am dying of curiosity now. *Who* is this lady of my court who has so enthralled you that you will have none other if you cannot have her? Tell me! You have my sworn word that I will tell no other person—man or woman."

Feeling that he could not express himself adequately in words, Alexandros mindspoke. After a moment, Mara's eyes first softened, then misted, and she reached out to take his calloused hand in both of hers.

"Lekos, oh, Lekos," she spoke aloud, a catch in her voice, "there is so much that you do not understand. If I make love to you, it will not be to you that I am making love. I will be reliving a physical contact that ended eighty years ago. Alexandros of Pahpahspolis was the Lekos I loved . . . and love still, though I saw him die forty years ago. And I was already ten times his age, even as we loved, though he knew it not.

"Dear Lekos, despite my appearance, I have lived for more than three hundred thirty years. From what you have said, you must be an Ehleen Christian. Know you not what your own priests say of such as me, that we are Satan's own folk, deathless sorcerers and witches, cursed by God? Are you not afraid of ensorcellment and eternal damnation?"

"I can see and feel nothing of evil in you, Mara," said Alexandroṣ bluntly. "As for the persecution of your kind by Christians, Father Vokos had an explanation that I have always remembered. He said that ignorant men, when faced with a person or situation or object they could not understand, first fear, then fear breeds hate, then a means is found to justify that hatred.

"Yes, Mara, I am a Christian. I care not about your age; I am a man and I desire the lovely woman you are . . . and I think you desire me, as well. So, what then stands in our path, Mara?"

Her gaze met him levelly. "Nothing, Lekos," she said simply.

9

Sub-lieutenant Stamos and his patrol, riding the left flank of the High King's army, clattered into a tiny, foothill village just before noon. They had crossed the Kuzahwahtchee River at dawn, so Stamos estimated that perhaps a quarter of the main force was now in Karaleenos.

This was the third little village they had entered, always after approaching through acre upon acre of ash and char, denoting crops burned where they stood. Stamos was glad they'd brought along feedbags for their mounts, since most of the grass and wild grains had also disappeared in the holocaust.

Stamos detached a galloper and sent him back to find Captain Portos and apprise that officer of the utter lack of forage in the fields. It was the second galloper so far; the first had been sent when they had come across the fourth polluted water source.

The sergeant came alongside and saluted. "If this place proves deserted, too, it might be a good halt for the noon, sir. At least there'll be some shade, if nothing else."

Sub-lieutenant Stamos nodded slightly, and the sergeant set about searching the huts and cabins and empty storehouses, but there was no living creature, not even a dog or a hen. Nor were there any portable items of value . . . and the men commenced to grumble, for loot had been their principal incentive for enlisting under King Zastros' Green Serpent Banner.

Stamos dismounted and strode to look down the stone-lined village well, unconsciously holding his breath against the expected reek of rotting flesh. About twenty feet down, however, the surface of the water was dark and still and the only things his nose registered were coolness and damp, mossy stones.

A man was sent down the narrow steps that spiraled around the inner wall to probe with his hook-backed lance, but all he brought into view were a couple of old, water-logged buckets and a few short lengths of rotting rope. So Stamos had a leather bucketful drawn, and then he stripped off a silver armlet and dunked it in. When the silver did not discolor—as, everyone knew, it would have, had the water been poisoned—he sipped a mouthful from his cupped hand, then jerked off his helmet and padded, sweat-soaked hood and dunked his head into the bucket.

Grinning through his dripping beard, he said, "If I'm not dead in a few minutes, Sergeant, have the men go ahead and water the horses. God, that stuff is cold!"

After the glare of the sun, the interior of the partially covered well was dark, so it was not the first or the second but the third trooper who chanced upon the "treasure." There, in a cooling niche that had been fashioned into the wall near the stairs, sat six stone jugs, each looking to hold about a half gallon. The trooper drew the corncob stopper and sniffed . . . and when he came back up, he carried his brimful bucket with exceeding care.

With their mounts watered and cared for, the sergeant designated a couple of troopers as sentries and, while the rest of the patrol settled down to their cold bacon and hard bread, he stumped over to join the officer at a table under a tree.

Stamos and the sergeant chewed stoically the same noisome fare as their troops in mutual silence. When they were done, he shared a small flask of wine with his grizzled second-in-command.

After a first sip of fine wine, the sergeant half turned and bawled for another pair of men to go and relieve the lookouts. There was no response. Grumbling about the lack of discipline in these modern-day armies, he rose from his stool and stumped around the well to the place where the troopers had gathered.

Suddenly he shouted in alarm, "Lieutenant Stamos, mount and ride! They're all dead! We've got to get out of . . . !" He grunted then, and Stamos heard the clashing of armor as he fell.

But before Stamos could reach his horse, he saw that he was surrounded. Short, fair warriors mounted on small, wild-looking horses now were spaced between the buildings, and detachments were trotting up the road.

Stamos cleared his throat. "Who is your leader?" He asked the question twice, first in Ehleeneekos, then in Merikan. When there was no answer, he added, "I am Lord Sub-lieutenant Stamos of Tchehrohkeespolis and the eldest son of my house. My father will pay a good ransom for my safe return."

"Sorry," said one of the horsemen, grinning, "we take no prisoners, Ehleen."

After a full day and no word from the far western patrol, Captain Portos dispatched a full troop—one-hundred-twenty troopers, six sergeants and three officers—on the route presumably taken by Stamos' men. They rode through a deserted countryside, peopled only by small, wild things; the only animals, larger than a rabbit, that any of them saw were a brace of wild turkeys pacing across a burned field, the sunlight striking a bronzed sheen from their plumage.

They took time to fire the structures of the two empty villages, so it was well into early afternoon when they entered the third. Out of no more than curiosity, a sergeant rode over to see what sort of offal this well contained . . . and the missing patrol was found.

Troop-Lieutenant Nikos was a veteran. After thoroughly searching the empty buildings, he posted three platoons in a tight, dismounted guard about the village perimeter, with another platoon standing to horse in a central location. The other two platoons were detailed to the grisly task of raising the bodies from the well.

When twenty nude corpses lay in ordered rows, Nikos examined them closely. Only four bore marks of violence:

young Stamos' skull had been cleft to the eyes by a sword blow; the wound in the sergeant's back had been made by an arrow; two of the troopers had had their throats cut. There was no single wound upon the cold flesh of any of the remaining sixteen!

Nikos sent his best tracker on a wide swing around the village and a trail was sighted, headed across the charred fields, due west, toward the mountains.

Nikos recalled the guard, mounted the troop, and trotted them to the wide swath of disturbed ashes. "How many?" he demanded of the tracker. "How long ago?"

Swinging from his saddle, the tracker eyed the trail critically, then switched the buzzing flies from a pile of horse droppings and thrust his finger into one of them, gauging the degree of warmth. "Between fifty and sixty horses, Lord Nikos, but not all bore riders. They are a day ahead of us."

"Were any of the horses ours?" asked Nikos needlessly, already knowing the answer.

"Close to half, Lord Nikos, bore shoes of our pattern. As for the shoe pattern of the other horses, which were smaller animals, I have never seen the like. They were not shaped by Karaleenoee," the tracker stated emphatically.

Nikos sighed. Nothing to be gained in following a day-old trail into unfamiliar territory with only one troop of light cavalry.

Returning to the village, they hastily distributed the score of corpses amongst the wooden houses, then fired them. They had only been on the return journey for a half hour, however, when suddenly, without warning, four troopers fell from their saddles, dead.

When it was pointed out to the troop-lieutenant that these had been the four men who labored in the depths of the well, affixing the ropes to corpse after cold corpse that their comrades might draw the burdens up, he brusquely ordered that none touch these bodies more. Leaving the men where they had fallen, he had the gear cut off their mounts, then set out for camp at a fast canter, his skin prickling under his armor at the thought of pestilence.

Despite King Zenos' fears of dissension, High Lord Milo's

horseclansmen and the mountain tribesmen of Karaleenos worked well and willingly together, far better than either group did with regular troops; their mutual dislike and distrust of the lowland Ehleenoee bound them together as much as did the war practices they shared and the fact that both faced a common foe.

A week after Troop-Lieutenant Nikos had frantically galloped his troop back to camp, three men squatted around a small fire near the mouth of a large cavern, chewing tough meat and tougher bread and washing down their fare with long drafts from a goatskin of resinous wine.

Tall, spare, and big-boned, Chief Hwahlt Hohlt's brown hair and beard showed streaks of gray, and nothing else betrayed his years, for he was possessed of a strength and endurance equal to that of his co-commanders.

He spoke: "Much as I hated to see thet good shine go down the gullets of them bastards, she worked like a charm—I'll say thet."

"Trust to an Ehleenoee to think of stealth and poison, rather than open battle and honest steel," growled Pawl Vawn of Vawn through a mouthful of mutton. But the twinkle in his hazel eyes revealed his words as banter, not insult.

Tomos Gonsalos took a swig of wine and grinned. "I thank both of you ratty-looking types for the compliments, if such they were. Sometimes it's hard to tell what you barbarians really mean."

"But what good did it do God-Milo to feed those troopers poisoned whisky?" put in the Vawn quizzically. "With their two miserable watchers downed, we could as easily have shafted most of them, then ridden in and sabered the rest. They'd have been just as dead."

Tomos questioned in answer. "Did you notice how Zastros narrowed his columns and stopped all patroling within leagues of that village, Pawl? Disease has killed more soldiers than all the steel ever forged, and they fear it in proportion.

"As to how this little scheme has aided King Zenos and High Lord Milo," he said, weighing the wineskin for a moment, "look at you, Pawl." And then he shot a thin stream of wine into the fire.

"Now, what would happen were I to now remove the nozzle from the mouth of the skin?"

Hwahlt answered, "All our wine would be in the fire and you'd find my knife blade kinda hard to digest."

Tomos ignored the mountaineer and continued. "My King and your High Lord need time, and the way we gave them some little time is this: the swamps extend far inland, near to that village, and Zastros is not fool enough to try to march troops and horsemen and haul wagons through the fens; therefore, it would appear that—as he needs to maintain a wide front to achieve any kind of speed of march—he originally intended to march both on the narrow strip of flatlands and in the foothills. But now that his troops are afraid that pestilence stalks those foothills . . . well," he said, squirting another stream of wine into the fire, "we've put a nozzle on his army just like the nozzle on this skin. So there's a stream going north, instead of a flood. Thus do we buy time for our lords."

To the east, across the width of that narrow strip of flatlands, Benee poled his flat-bottomed boat through the ways known only to his fellow swampfolk. His skinny body was nearly nude and he was smeared from head to foot with mud. He beached his boat with a barely audible crunch on a tiny sandspit at the foot of a high, grassy bank. Taking a small, wooden cylinder from the bottom of the boat, he entered the grass and slithered up the slope as silently as a cottonmouth . . . and every bit as deadly.

Just below the rim, he stretched out on his back and fitted the sections of his blowpipe together, then carefully inserted a two-inch dart, its needlepoint smeared with a viscous substance.

Gingerly, he parted the small bushes clinging to the edge of the slope and his keen eyes judged the distance between him and the nearest spearman, who slowly paced to and fro, his frequent yawns loud to Benee's ears. No, the distance was just too far for a sure hit on vulnerable flesh, and blowdarts could seldom pierce cloth, much less armor.

Up . . . and over the edge, a shadow among the shadows. Flat as the earth itself, his supple body conformed to every

hump or hollow of the ground it covered. Two yards closer
. . . five yeards, and Benee could pick out a movement of the
sentry's arm, accompanied by rasp of clothing and muttered
curse as he scratched himself.

Six yards closer, then seven, eight, and Benee stopped,
stockstill, fear suddenly drying his mouth, sucking the air
from his lungs. The sentry had turned and was looking dead
ahead at him! He fought the almost overwhelming urge to get
up and run, run, run, back to the safety of the boat, of the
swamps of his birth. But that way lay certain death; already
could he feel that spear blade in his back.

Then, all was again well. Muttering something incompre-
hensible under his breath, the man began to pace back and
forth, but never more than a few yards in any direction.

At the end of thirty agonizing feet, Benee felt he could be
accurate enough for a sure kill. Slowly, he brought up his
blowpipe, made certain that the war dart was still in place,
then put it to his lips and took exacting aim. A single puff of
his powerful, trained lungs . . . and death flew toward the
nameless spearman.

The sentry slapped at his cheek, as if at an insect. But
when his fingers felt the dart and his mind registered what it
must be, he screamed! Screaming on and on, regularly, like a
woman at a birthing, he dropped his spear and ran a few
strides toward the distant firelight. All at once, he stopped
screaming and fell, his limbs jerking and twitching.

But Benee had not been idle. As soon as the spear was
dropped, he ran forward at a crouch and scooped it up; still
at a crouching run, he reached the lip of the bank and was
over it before the sentry fell. He took time to disassemble his
blowpipe and fit the sections back into their cylinder, then
slung it and loped down to his boat.

Before he pushed off, he gently placed the spear in the
boat. Tonight, Benee had become a full man, and this spear
was proof of the fact.

So, along the fringes of that narrow land, the swampers
and the mountain bands took regular toll of Zastros' troops,
never many at one time. But the constant threat of ambush

began to retard an already snail-slow advance, as the exposed flanks unconsciously drew closer to the center.

So Zastros had two columns of light infantry sent into a particularly troublesome stretch of fenland and no officer or man of them was ever seen again. The harrassment never even slowed. The next unit was a full *tahgmah* of Zastros' picked men. Two long weeks later, a bare two hundred of that thousand staggered or crawled out of the fens, and most of those survivors were useless as soldiers, what with strange fevers and festered wounds and addled wits.

And the march route was officially narrowed again, keeping a couple of miles between the eastern flank and the edges of the fens. And Zastros raged and swore at these additional delays. And his young queen, Lilyuhn, whom some named "Witch," listened to his tirades in heavy-lidded, expressionless silence.

Captain Portos rode back from the High King's camp in a towering rage. His quite reasonable request that his battered, now understrength, unit be replaced on the hazardous left flank had been coolly denied. As if that were not enough, his personal courage had been questioned for having the temerity to make such a request, and then the High King had refused him his right to meet the questioner at swordpoints.

How quickly, he pondered, did kings forget. When the High King—then *Thohooks* Zastros, with only a distant claim to the throne—first had raised the banner of rebellion, *Komees* Portos had enlisted and armed and mounted a squadron of light horses and taken up the rebel cause. Most of that first squadron had been recruited of his own city and lands. Then, oh, then, Zastros had warmly embraced him, spoken to and of him as "brother," sworn undying gratitude and rich rewards for such aid.

Portos had watched most of that first squadron extirpated at the Battle of Ahrbahkootchee, and he had fled with Zastros across the dread border into the Great Southern Swamp, within which, somewhere, lay the Witch Kingdom. What with fevers and quicksands and horrible, deadly animals, he had had but a bare score left when Zastros sent word to him and the other living officers. And Portos and his score, all with high prices on their heads, had returned to the ancestral lands and secretly raised and armed and mounted another squadron.

Then came first the horrifying word that King Rahndos and seven other claimants to the throne had, all in one day, *deliberately slain themselves*! *Thoheeks* Fahrkos, who had no more right to the throne than Zastros, had been crowned. Then had the kingdom been well and truly split asunder as a host of pretenders' warbands marched north and south and east and west, fighting each other as often as they fought Fahrkos. Cities were besieged or felled by storm, villages were burned; noble and peasant alike fled to mountain and forest and swamp, as fire and rapine and slaughter stalked the land in clanking armor.

Portos and most of Zastros' other captains defended their lands as best they could, stoutly held their cities, and awaited word from the Witch Kingdom, where dwelt their lord.

They waited for three long years, while the once-mighty, once-wealthy Southern Kingdom dissolved around them into a hodgepodge myriad of small, ever-warring statelets. Fahrkos ruled his capital and controlled a few miles of land around it, but a large proportion of his predecessor's fine army had left with many of his most powerful lords, when they departed to cast their hats into the much-crowded ring. The strong central government that had made the Southern Kingdom what it had been and extended its borders over the years had collapsed into anarchy and chaos; from the western savannas to the eastern saltfens, from the Iron Mountains to the Great Southern Swamp, might made right and the status of men was determined not by their pedigree, but by the strength of their swordarm and the size of their warband.

At last the long-deferred summons came and Portos led his squadron to the rendezvous, leaving defense of his lands and city in the hands of his two younger brothers. By the time Zastros and his Witch Kingdom bride, the Lady Lilyuhn arrived, there were fifteen thousand armed men to greet them . . . and a full tenth of that force was Portos' squadron.

Portos and all the rest had expected an immediate, lightning drive on the ill-defended capital, but Zastros marched them west, bearing north, through the very heart of the savannas onto the shores of the King of Rivers; and men marveled at the size of his force—the largest seen under one banner since the breakup of King Fahrkos' inherited army—and noble and peasant alike came from fen and from forest to take their oaths to so obviously powerful a leader . . . only such a one as he could put things right again.

Then it was north and east for the more than doubled army, and petty claimants—who might have had a bare chance against equally unworthy opposition—saw the death of glorious pipedreams and swore their allegiances to Zastros and added their warbands to his, so that, by the time he camped below the walls of Seetheerospolis, the fifty thousand men under his banner left the *Eeyehgeestan* of the Iron Mountains no choice but to throw their far from inconsiderable forces and resources into Zastros' lap. And the massive army marched due south, again bypassing the capital, then east to the fringes of the saltfens.

Only when he had almost seven times his beginning strength did he turn toward the capital and King Fahrkos, whom he considered a traitor, since Fahrkos had been one of his supporters in his first rebellion. As Zastros' van came within the crown lands, the pitiful remnant of that mighty force that had trampled his aspirations into the gory mud of Ahrbahkootchee only five years agone threw down their battered arms, hailed him savior of the realm, and begged leave to serve him.

King Fahrkos, even his advisors and bodyguard having deserted to Zastros, slew his wife, his daughters, and his young son, then fired the wing that had housed his loved family, and fell on his sword. Only the prompt arrival of Zastros' huge army prevented the entire palace complex from burning.

So the victorious Zastros was crowned High King of all Ehleenoee, a new title, never before claimed by any other. But to the faithful Portos, the price of victory had been steep. Soon after his squadron's departure, his city had been stormed, sacked, and razed by some bannerless warband; only the citadel had successfully resisted, but both his brothers had died in the defense. And what with disease and accident and the occasional skirmish, no troop of his squadron could, on Coronation Day, muster more than fifty men.

But when Zastros announced his intention of taking advantage of the war betwixt Karaleenos and Kehnooryos Ehlahs to reunite all the Ehleenoee under his rule, ever-faithful Portos did what he felt he must: he sold his ancestral lands and what was left of his city for what little he could get—and that was little enough; considering the condition of the kingdom, more than he'd expected, really—and he re-armed, re-equipped, and recruited replacements to flesh out the shrunken squadron.

Since then, his men had been first to set hoof upon the soil of Karaleenos, had been first to die from hostile action, had ridden nowhere other than van or scout or extended flank. In five weeks he had lost nearly six hundred irreplaceable men and almost as many horses, all by enemy action or disease. Also, being stationed where they were, his troops were at the very tail of the supply lines; therefore, they wanted for everything. His loyal officers and sergeants drove themselves and their troops relentlessly, but it seemed that each order from Zastros' pavilion was more stupidly impossible than the last. And Portos could feel it in his bones: there would be a mutiny—and soon!—if something were not done to raise the morale of his battered squadron.

That was the reason he had ridden the dusty miles to the main camp, to ask the lord, for whom he had sacrificed so much for so many years, that what was left of his command be *temporarily* shifted from their hazardous position, be replaced by another squadron long enough to resupply and restore the morale of the men. And he had been spurned like a homeless cur, been kept waiting for hours—a dusty pariah among the well-fed, well-groomed officers, whose burnished armor bore not one nick or scratch.

Anger had finally taken over and he had forced his way into first the anteroom, then the audience chamber, swatting aside gaudy officers and adjutants and aides-de-camp as if they had been annoying insects. The pikemen of the King's bodyguard knew Captain Portos of old and did not try to bar his entrance.

Portos shuddered strongly and his lips thinned to a grim

line when once more he thought on the things that had been said to him . . . and *of* him, a veteran officer, of proven loyalty and courage . . . in that chamber. The only thing of which he could now be certain was that the King Zastros who had not only heaped insult and unwarranted abuse upon him, but allowed—nay, *encouraged*—others to do the same, was not the Zastros for whom he, Portos, had led more than twenty-four hundred brave men to their deaths and willingly forfeited his last meager possessions! Perhaps that wife he had taken unto himself during the years he dwelt in the Witch Kingdom had ensorcelled him.

But, ensorcelled or not, Portos resolved, ere he reached his own camp, that never again would his men suffer or his sacred honor be questioned by Zastros.

10

The cyclopean masonry of the Luhmbuh River bridge had weathered hundreds of years of floods and at least one titanic earthquake, so Milo had not been surprised when both his artificers and King Zenos' despaired of doing it any damage not easily repairable. On the fords, however, he was luckier. The more treacherous of the two, thirty miles upstream, was found to be natural; but the better one, only twelve miles west of the bridge, was manmade of large blocks of granite. Milo had both ends dismantled, rafting the stones downstream to help fortify the northern end of the bridge.

With the arrival of *Strahteegos* Gabos and the main Confederation army, things began to hum. The fledgling *castra* was completed in a day, then much enlarged and elaborated upon, though compartmentalized for easy defense by a small force.

It had been his idea to send the Maklaud and his horse-clansmen to help King Zenos' mountain irregulars and reports indicated that they made a good combination.

By the end of the four weeks, Milo was heartened. Not only had Zastros' speed been reduced to a slow crawl that promised precious time, but the first condottas from the Middle Kingdoms were arriving—horsemen all, armored in half suits of plate, armed with lance, sword, shield, and dirk; every fourth trooper being an expert horse-archer and bearing a powerful hornbow. The condottas averaged small—five hundred being an exceptionally large unit—but these

107

Freefighters were the best soldiers of this era. They were versatile, highly mobile, and courageous, if well-led.

The middle of the sixth week brought the gallant old Duke of Kuhmbuhlun, at the head of his own army of six thousand, plus the promised sixty-five hundred from Pitzburk. There was word, as well, from the King of Harzburk. Not to be outdone by his arch-rival of Pitzburk, he was sending *six* hundred noble cavalry and seven thousand Freefighters . . . as soon as he could find and hire them.

By chance, Milo and some of his staff happened to be standing near the west gate of the *castra* when another column of light cavalry trotted in . . . with Tomos Gonsalos, who was supposed to be helping lead the harassment in the southern mountains, riding knee to knee with an unknown Ehleen officer at their head. Milo mindspoke Tomos, who spoke a word or two to his companion, then turned his dusty mount toward the High Lord.

"What have we here, Tomos?" Milo spoke aloud, since not all his party were talented with mindspeak. "If that condotta are irregulars, they're the best armed and disciplined irregulars I've ever seen; if they're Freefighters, they're a draggle-tailed lot. And I thought you rode south with Maklaud."

Tomos grinned engagingly. "I'm not really needed there, Lord Milo. Your Lordship was right, the Horseclansmen and King Zenos' mountain warriors are of the same coinage; they blend as easily as hot cheese and butter." But, even while speaking lightly aloud, he imparted more serious information by mindspeak. "There are nearly a thousand veteran light cavalry here, the personal squadron of Captain Portos over there. They are topnotch troops, and I know, my lord, for we've been skirmishing with them for over a month."

"*Deserters?*" Milo looked his astonishment. "These were Zastros' troops?"

"Among his best, my lord, *Komees* Portos has captained cavalry in Zastros' behalf for six years, since first he raised his banner. He has lost or sold everything he owned in Zastros' cause."

Milo shook his head. "At best, turncoats are unreliable, and a thousand possibly hostile horsemen in my camp is more than I care to risk. We'd best have them disarmed. We can put the troopers to work. I'll send the officers, under guard, up to Kehnooryos Atheenahs with the next . . ."

"Your pardon, my lord," interrupted Tomos. "But I have reason to believe Captain *Komees* Portos' story and . . ."

"And," snapped Milo, "you are a very young man, but men far older have been deluded."

"And," Tomos continued, "I was instructed by the Maklaud to inform Your Lordship that the captain had been subjected to the Test of the Cat and found completely truthful. He also said that Your Lordship should hear the tale and put your own questions to the captain."

"And so," concluded Portos, "when I reached my camp, I told my officers what had happened at the High King's camp and what I intended doing. I did not need to tell them what would happen if the squadron remained under the High King's orders. Then I mounted a fresh horse and rode into the mountains with a white pennon on my lanceshaft. It required nearly two days for me to make contact. When at last I did, I asked to meet with their chiefs.

"Chief Maklaud seemed to believe me from the start, but Chief Hohlt and Tomos, here, were quite skeptical. Tomos suggested putting me to the torture, that I might reveal my nefarious schemes; Chief Hohlt was in favor of simply slitting my throat."

"So the Maklaud explained the Test of the Cat, then had you submit to it," added Milo, smiling, smiling because he knew, as had the Maklaud, that such a test was completely unnecessary with a man like the captain, who lacking mindspeak, also lacked a mindshield. Milo's already-high estimation of the Maklaud went up; he had employed his prairie cat and a bit of showmanship to keep secret his ability to read some minds.

"All right, Captain Portos, if you wish to sign on your condotta, I pay good wages. But there will be no foraging; let that be understood now. My supply trains arrive twice a week, it's plain fare, but you'll not be shorted by *my* quartermasters. Under normal conditions, I pay Freefighter captains half the agreed wages when I hire them, but I saw your squadron when they rode in. So, would you rather have your advance in equipment, Captain?"

Since most Ehleenoee were far less prone to evidencing emotion than were Horseclansmen, Milo was genuinely surprised to see tears come into the big captain's eyes. But when he answered, his voice was firm. "My lord is more than generous. It has . . . pained me for weeks to see my men suffer for lack of those things that a captain should be able to provide, but the initial expense of bringing my squadron back up to strength took every bit of the gold my lands brought, so I had nothing to bribe the quartermasters. Then, when your horse-archers raided my camp that night and fired our supply wagons . . ."

Milo tentatively probed Portos' mind, but he hurriedly withdrew with a lump in his throat; in that moment, the High Lord felt real hate for Zastros, that his hauteur and neglect toward one who had served him faithfully and long had reduced that proud and honorable man to what he—Portos—considered the acceptance of charity. For the first time, Milo really noticed the southern nobleman's appearance—the old and battered helmet with half the crest long since hacked away, the patched and repatched clothing and boots, the cheap scale-mail hauberk, where most officers and nobles wore plate. And he came to a decision that he was never to regret.

He raised his voice, calling, "Lieutenant Markos."

Shortly, a small, heavy chest rested beside his chair. On the tabletop were an ewer of wine and four cups, and another chair had been brought in.

After the aide had left in search of *Strahteegos* Gabos, Milo turned to Tomos. "I think that Captain Portos and I are about of a size. Go over into my quarters and tell my men to open my chests, then choose some clothing and boots suitable for a captain of a thousand horse, then have them bring your choices and my extra suit of Pitzburk back here."

As Tomos rose to go, the big captain protested, "But, my lord . . . I ask only for those who depend upon me, not for myself."

"Because, in addition to being a born leader and true gentleman, you're a really good officer, and that, my good Portos, is a far rarer combination than you think; too many officers, especially nobleborn officers, remember only that

'Rank Hath Its Privileges,' forgetting that 'Rank Hath Its Responsibilities,' as well. You gave more than your all to one who betrayed your trust. You must now be very cynical regarding the gratitude of rulers, but I say to you this: serve me as faithfully as you served Zastros in the past, and the rewards for both you and your squadron will be great."

While Portos sat digesting the unexpected praise, Milo leaned to open the small coffer and extract three leather bags that he dropped, clanking, on the table, then shoved over to Portos.

"Captain, we maintain and enforce high standards of personal cleanliness in our army, especially amongst our officers, so you will need more than a single suit of clothes; the smaller bag is for your own needs. With the two larger bags, I expect you to improve the appearances of your officers, nor will you have to search far, for—impending battle or no impending battle—a host of sutlers and merchants have opened for business along both sides of the road just north of the *castra*, along with armorers, tailors, whores, pimps, gamblers, bootmakers, horsetraders, farriers, fortune-tellers, and thieves. God help them all if we lose the battle!"

"*No*, my lord!" Portos shook his head emphatically. "The supplies for my troopers are more important. In honor, I cannot accept . . ."

"*Captain Portos*!" Milo snapped. "In *my* army you will accept what I damn well tell you to accept. Your sergeants and troopers will be supplied by my quartermaster with whatever they need, be it clothing or weapons or armor or horses or blankets or even cookpots. And Sacred Sun help the quartermaster I ever apprehend cadging bribes for preferential issuance of stores!"

Then Tomos and Milo's orderlies arrived and, by the time Gabos came puffing in, Captain *Komees* Portos looked the part of a noble officer—black, thigh-length boots; breeches and shirt of plum-colored linen canvas; black leather gambeson under a three-quarter suit of matchless Pitzburk plate.

Without preliminaries, Milo said, "Gabos, ever since you became Senior *Strahteegos*, you've been badgering me to train and allot you more Ehleen cavalry, despite the fact that—as you well know—my efforts along that line have been dismal failures for reasons we'll not here recite.

"Well, to your right sits the answer to your prayers. His name is Portos, he is a *Kath'ahróhs* and a *Komees* by birth, he commands nine hundred sixty-eight veteran lancers, all Ehleenoee. Until recently, his unit served in the army of King Zastros, who shamelessly misused him and them. Tomos has fought Portos' troopers and he considers them first-rate opponents, brave, and well led. Do you want them?"

Gabos turned and eyed Portos shrewdly, then snapped coldly, "Why did you desert your former lord, *Komees* Portos?"

Crisply and succinctly, Portos told him. While he spoke, Gabos mindspoke the High Lord, "You believe this tale, Lord Milo?"

"Yes," Milo answered silently. "I have entered his mind, and so has the Maklaud. He has been completely candid with us all."

"I like his bearing," commented Gabos, "and he speaks and expresses himself well. Yes, I'll take him and his men as regulars. I'd be a bigger fool than I am not to, Lord Milo."

"Than say it aloud," ordered Milo. "The good captain doesn't mindspeak."

Pale moonlight bathed Lord Alexandros' couch and a soft night breeze cooled his love-wet skin. Mara lay pressed close beside him, her head pillowed on his shoulder, her breath still ragged, her shapely legs quivering yet from the joy he had given her.

After a long, dreamy while, she half whispered, "Lekos?"

"Yes, Mara?" he murmured.

Without speaking, she rolled her body atop his, her full, firm breasts pressed tightly against his chest. Resting on her elbows, her thick hair cascaded down either side of her small head, enclosing their two faces in a faery-pavilion through which moonlight filtered as through blue-black gossamer. For an interminable moment, she gazed into his eyes, then slowly lowered her face and pasted her hot, red mouth firmly over his. But when his arms made to close around her, she tore out of their incipient embrace.

"No, Lekos, we must talk."

Knowing her moodiness as well as he knew her matchless body, Alexandros lay back, cupping his hands beneath his head.

Mara reclined on her elbow, tracing the scars on his body with a forefinger. Keeping her eyes firmly fixed on the finger, she stated. "Lekos, I love you. I think that I love you as much as I loved your grandfather, my first Lekos . . . perhaps more. With you, in these past weeks, I have re-experienced a rapture that I had thought I would never again know.

"But, unlike my first Lekos, *you* as well as I knew that it could not last, that it must end. And why, as well. I would gladly give anything of which I can think if you could be as me or I as you, but Fate has ruled otherwise.

"My husband and Aldora and I are not truly immortal—Demetrios' death proves that. Anything that keeps air from our lungs is fatal to us, but our almost-instantaneous regeneration of tissue makes us impervious to most injuries or wounds or diseases and keeps us youthful for hundreds of years. To look at Aldora or at me, few would guess our ages at over five-and-twenty, yet Aldora is well past her fiftieth year, and I am well over three hundred years old. Milo is not even certain of his own age; he thinks that he is seven hundred, possibly more.

"What I am trying to tell you, Lekos . . ."

Gently, he placed two fingers to her full lips and softly said, "That you could not bear to see me grow old, my Mara? No, that must never happen, my love, for it would be the cruelest of torture for both of us. So you wish me to leave. When must I leave you?"

"I dispatched a galley this morning, Lekos. With favorable weather, she should reach Kehnooryos Knossos in a few days. The message I sent Captain Yahnekos was to send a larger ship than a bireme . . . for I have a favor to ask you, Lekos."

"And what is that, Mara?"

"I want you to take Aldora with you, Lekos. Knowing her proclivities, she'll no doubt seduce you soon after you reach home . . . if not before. But make love to her with a free heart, Lekos, for my blessing will be upon you both."

This time, it was Mara whose hand covered his mouth, stilling his outraged protests.

"Be still, Lekos, and listen well. Long life does not equate to eternal happiness. Aldora has had a tragic life to date. She was born of a noble family of Theesispolis and her father was of the sort of *Vahrohnos* Paulos, whom you slew; his wife was a necessary evil, because he could breed no sons without a woman. When poor Aldora was but a babe, her mother died and you can imagine how much parental affection a girl-child received from such a father. She grew to be a bigger than average girl and became pubescent at about ten. When she was but eleven, Theesispolis was taken by storm and she had to watch her father and brothers butchered by mercenaries, three of whom later raped her, then sold her to a horseclansman who did not speak her language. At that time, her mindspeak talent was quiescent. Horseclansmen share their concubines and sometimes their wives with their kindred or eminent guests, and I'll not elaborate on her ordeal before it was brought to the attention of the clansmen that, since the girl was less than fourteen, they were violating a tribal law in using her.

"Before it was done, that clan's chief was deposed and slain, and her erstwhile owner became chief in his stead. Then he did what he could to recompense her. Being told that her real father was dead, he adopted her as his own daughter—rapist turned father, you see.

"For a few years after Milo and Demetrios formed the Confederation and became joint High Lords, Demetrios gave every indication of wishing to be like Milo in all ways. Demetrios, it was, who suggested marriage to Aldora. By that time, she was nearing sixteen and had become the complete Horseclanswoman.

"Do not, Lekos, confuse Ehleen maidens with Horseclans 'maidens.' After they are fourteen, girls of the clans are allowed just as much sexual freedom as the boys. Pregnant brides are, to a Horseclansman, a normal occurrence; virgin brides are unheard of.

"Aldora had been taking full and very frequent advantage

of the custom of the tribe, so she was far from inexperienced when Milo and I finally browbeat her into marrying Demetrios. For a few months, they seemed happy enough, but then he reverted to type. He fell madly in love with one of his aides. Aldora chanced to catch the two of them at it one day, and the fat was in the fire!

"Since that day, she has seduced most of the court—with the exception of Demetrios' and Paulos' clique, though she did rub her husband's face in the fact that she'd seduced one of his own lovers—army officers, Freefighter captains, country gentry. And recently, since Demetrios' remains were found, she's attended a few of Lady Ioanna's frolics. I just want to get the girl out of this reeking court and among normal, honest, uncomplicated fighting men," she said, squeezing his arm, "like you, dearest."

"I think," said Alexandros coldly, "that the woman is a bit shopworn for my taste. But if you truly want me to take her to the Sea Isles, she'll certainly not lack for those to play stallion. I am more discriminating than most of my men."

"Lekos," she asked softly, "do you consider me to be shopworn, as well?"

"Now, by God, Mara!" He sat up and grabbed her shoulders roughly, anger and hurt mingling in his voice. "You *know* that I said not a word concerning you. I love you, Mara; if God wills that I live to be an old man with a long, white beard, I still will love you and treasure in my old man's memory the joy and the beauty we shared for so short a time.

"But, my love, I harbor no wish to be but the most recent in your precious Aldora's long, long, *long* string of seductions. Can't you see? Can't you understand?"

"Lekos, Milo can explain this better than can I, for he has much of the knowledge from the times of the Old Ones, the godlike men who once owned this world before their weapons of wizardry destroyed them. Nonetheless, I'll try to tell it to you as he has told it to me . . . he knows her mind, has explored it deeply, both he and Aldora possessing mental talents that I, alas, lack.

"Lekos, for the first ten years of her life, Aldora was denied any semblance of a father's love, something Milo says is of vital importance to a girl-child. He says that what she is unconsciously seeking is a father to love her and protect her and care for her, as well as a sexual partner to assuage her carnal needs; ideally, what she needs is a vigorous older man, but there lie the three walls that entrap her. The first wall is the thickest and is well below her conscious mind; its ponderous stones are fears—very well justified, considering her ordeal—of the brutal and terrifying degradation of rape, mortared with a vague and confused horror of incest.

"The second wall is the highest, and it is a wall that confronts all of our kind. She seeks a man of forty to forty-five years, but even if she could somehow break down that first wall, she could not surmount the second—not on the basis of permanence that she also craves. For, Lekos, how many *men* live much beyond sixty years?

"The third wall is my husband, Milo. Aldora both loves and deeply respects him—though, for some reason, she tries hard not to show these feelings publicly. But, having watched her grow up and having helped to educate her, having shown her how to develop and properly channel her prodigious mental talents, he feels fatherly toward her. Consequently, he has been able to resist her wiles all these years. Too, he is armed with the predictions of dear old Blind Harri, who was Aldora's other teacher."

"Blind Harri?" asked Alexandros. "One of your kind or one of mine?"

Mara shrugged. "One of yours . . . I think. But not even Milo or Harri himself knew for certain. He was at least one hundred thirty, when first Milo met him; he was twenty years older when Milo and I found each other. He migrated east with the tribe, but after Ehlai had been settled, he grew homesick for the plains and none could deter him from returning to them and to the scattered clans still living on them. With him went two-thirds of the Cat Clan. Their breed is not really suited to this region.

"As last living member of his clan, Blind Harri bore the rank of Chief, but he was much more than that, Lekos, and very powerful within the tribe. And his mental abilities were stronger and more numerous than even Milo's or Aldora's. Among other powers was the ability to, under rare conditions, see the future with astounding accuracy.

"Before he rode back west, about twenty-five years ago, he imparted to Milo and me a number of predictions concerning the futures of the Confederation and of various clans mostly. But he said of Aldora, 'Her husband, who cannot live as a man, will at least die as a man should; it will be many long years ere she finds happiness, nor will it be in this land, but beyond many salty seas.' "

"Very well, Mara, I'll take the Lady Aldora out onto the first of those salty seas. But ask no more."

Taking his hand, she kissed the palm. "Thank you, Lekos. But I must ask more. I must ask that you be kind to her, for she was suffering years before you were born, and she will be suffering yet when your wonderful splendid body is dust."

In a husky voice he inquired, "And will you remember my body, Mara? When I am dust, will you remember me?"

And he was immediately rueful of his words in the sight of the tears coursing down her cheeks. The words she tried to speak came only as gasping sobs.

"Mara, dearest, please forgive me. I'd not deliberately hurt you, never, you know that."

Gathering her into his arms, he cradled her shuddering body against his own, crooning soothing words he could never recall, until at last grief became exhaustion, and exhaustion became sleep.

11

From the day of the mass defection of Captain Portos' squadron, the Karaleenos guerrillas and Horseclansmen were careful to leave unmolested the troops whose flank he had been guarding, though they kept these troops under constant surveillance, sometimes dressing the darker-haired men in lancer uniforms and having them ride captured horses. They kept to this routine until the return of Tomos Gonsalos. Then he, Hohlt, and Vawn made their plans and marshaled their men.

Viewed from the night-cloaked mountains, Zastros' vast army was invisible. All that could be seen were myriad pinpricks of light, cooking fires, and watchfires. The observers knew that men sat and hunkered about those fires, eating, drinking, talking, laughing, grousing, gambling. But seen from the high hills, the plain might well have been but another section of night sky, filled with dim and flaring stars.

As the columns wound down through the hidden passes and secret ways, then converged under the loaf-shaped hill that had been designated their rendezvous point, the twinkling panorama disappeared and dark night enfolded them.

Staff-Lieutenant Foros Hedaos walked his horse behind the two trotting, torch-bearing infantrymen, sitting stiffly erect as an officer should in the performance of his duties, for Foros was a man who took his duties and himself very seriously. That was why he was riding the midnight rounds rather than leaving so irksome a detail to a guard-sergeant, as any of his peers would have done.

Behind him trotted the relief guard; Sergeant Crusos was at their head. Beneath his breath, the sergeant was cursing. Why did he have to draw this damned Foros as guard-officer? Even his fellow-officers thought him an ass, him and his "An officer should . . ." and "An officer shouldn't . . ." If the pock-faced bastard had stayed back in camp like any normal officer would have, Sergeant Crusos would be on horseback, not hoofing it along like a common pikeman!

Then they were at post number thirteen, and the officer reined aside, that Crusos might bring his men up. "Detail," hissed Crusos, "*halt*! Ground, *pikes*!"

"I really think, Sergeant," snapped Foros peevishly, "that you could make your commands a little more audible."

"Sir," began Crusos, "we're on enemy land and . . ."

Foros' face—deeply scarred by smallpox, beardless and ugly at the best of times—became hard and his voice took on a threatening edge. "Do not presume to argue with *me*, Sergeant! Just do as I command."

Then there came a loud splashing from within the deep-cut creekbed a bare hundred yards to their right, and the moon slipped from her cloudcover long enough to reveal a body of horsemen coming over the lip of the bank.

Sergeant Crusos' action then was instinctive. Full-throatedly, he roared, "Right *face*! Unsling, *shields*! Front rank, *kneel*! Post, *pikes*!"

"*Sergeant*!" screamed Foros, angrily. "What do you think you're doing?"

Crusos spun about and saluted with his drawn sword. "Sir, the detail is formed to repel cavalry attack."

"Oh, really, Sergeant." Foros smiled scornfully. "You're behaving like a frightened old woman. Bring the men back to marching order this minute. *I* saw those riders, and they had lances. That means they're Captain Portos' men."

It was in Crusos' mind to say that, in his time, he'd seen more *unfriendly* lancers than friendly; but he bit his tongue, remembering that the last noncom who had publicly disputed one of this officer's more questionable orders had been flogged and reduced to the ranks . . . that was one of the benefits of having married a daughter of the regimental commander, Martios.

When Tomos Gonsalos, trotting at the van of his platoon
of "lancers," heard the familiar commands and saw the
knife-edged pikeheads come slanting down, his hand unconsciously sought his saber hilt and he breathed a silent
prayer—the success of the entirety of this raid lay in not having to fight until the bulk of the raiders were at or near the
camp. Then the menacing points rose on command, shields
were reslung, and pikeshafts sloped over shoulders.

At the perimeter, Tomos raised a hand to halt his platoon,
then walked his mount over to where the infantry officer sat
stiff in his saddle.

"A fine evening, is it not?" said Tomos, smiling. "I am
Sub-lieutenant Manos Stepastios. Could you tell me, sir, if
this is the *Vahrohnos* Martios' camp?"

"No," the officer sneered. "It's the High King's seraglio!
Don't you know how to salute a superior?"

Hastily, Manos/Tomos rendered the demanded courtesy,
which the infantry officer returned . . . after a long, insulting
pause.

"That's better. Now, what are you and your aggregation of
tramps-in-armor doing this far east?" His voice was cold and
the sneer still on his ugly face.

Manos/Tomos remained outwardly courteous to the point
of servility, though his instinct was to drive his dirk into the
prominent Adam's apple under that pock-marked horseface.
"Sir, Captain Portos commanded me to ride to your camp to
discover if aught had been seen of the supply wagons. If not,
I was to speak to your supply officer."

The pocked officer laughed harshly, humorlessly. "So, Portos is begging again, is he? It's a complete mystery to me
why any, save barbarians, would serve a ne'er-do-well like
Captain Portos . . . but then," again, that cold, sneering
smile, "you are not exactly a *Kath'ahróhs*, westerner."

Manos/Tomos had had enough; furthermore, five hoots of
an "owl" had just sounded—all was in readiness. He approached until he was knee to knee with the arrogant officer,
then grated, "My Lady Mother was the daughter of a tribal
chief and was married to my noble father by the rites of the
Church. Are you equally legitimate, you ugly whoreson? If

the syphilitic sow who farrowed you knew your father's name, why have you refrained from identifying your house?"

Sergeant Crusos was very glad that, like his detail, he was still facing out into the dark, so broad was his grin. Someone had finally told off the supercilious swine! He was still grinning when the arrow buried itself in his chest.

The pikemen and torch bearers never had a chance and their few gasps of surprise or agony could not have been heard in the camp a hundred yards distant. As for Staff-Lieutenant Foros, he was still red-faced and spluttering, too outraged even to speak, when Tomos' hard-swung saber took off his ugly head.

Two thousand horsemen swept into the sleeping camp. Sabers slashed tent ropes and arrows pin-cushioned the heaving canvases before torches were tossed onto them. The guards at the commander's pavilion died messily, under lance and dripping sword blade. The *Vahrohnos* Martios, too besotted to even draw steel, was split from shoulder to breastbone by Chief Hohlt's broadsword.

Knots of two or three grim riders fanned out after the initial charge, ruthlessly shooting or lancing or slashing at any figure afoot, while select details put the torch to wagons or looted useful supplies and hastily packed them on captured horses and mules.

When he had seen the pack train well on its way, Tomos tapped his bugler's shoulder and the recall was sounded, while the Vawn mindcalled his Horseclansmen. The bugler had to repeat his notes three times, ere the raiders ceased of riding down screaming, weaponless foemen and reassembled. By that time, long columns of torches could be seen approaching from both south and east.

As the last of the exhausted, blood-soaked, but exultant horsemen headed back toward the mountains, Tomos, Hohlt, and Vawn surveyed the fiery, gory acres that had been camp to four thousand pikemen.

"We'd better get back and prepare the main passes," remarked Tomos conversationally. "Picking off scouts or stragglers is one thing, but for the morale of the rest of his army, Zastros is going to have to send retaliatory columns after *us*."

And they rode off in the wake of their men.

Milo's huge *castra* was already too small for the heterogeneous forces that were still responding. Almost every prin-
cipality in the Middle Kingdoms was represented, though
only one other had been able to match in size the forces of
Harzburk and Pitzburk. The Princes' Council of Eeree had
dispatched some thousand mounted axmen and sent word
that five thousand heavy infantry were on the march. And
Milo might have begun to entertain thoughts of meeting Zastros in open battle, were it not for that ambiguous prophecy.

Sitting alone in his pavilion, the volume of his private jour-
nal that contained the list of prophecies open before him,
Milo shook his head slowly. Old Harri had been amazingly
accurate in predicting future events, but the High Lord would
be far happier if the man of powers had worded his forewarn-
ings less bardically and more specifically.

> The hosts of the south will come in due time,
> Led by two bodies that share but one mind.
> But hold well, God-Milo, cross not the river,
> And the tribe, from ancient evil deliver.

So he refused all blandishments of his captains and his allies to erect any sort of serious fortifications south of the
bridge, though he did authorize a scattering of the more
suicidally inclined troops to establish and occupy small strong
points, with orders to retreat in the face of any really deter-
mined opposition . . . if they could.

Captain Portos had proved a goldmine of information.
First, in the matter of the elephants: Zastros had only eight
of the beasts, two of which were being used for nothing more
martial than to draw his huge headquarters wagon. Portos
had served both against and with the big animals and he assured Milo that, while they had been trained to use their
long, immensely strong noses to hurl stones and darts, and
while their charge could crumple any formation of pikemen
or other infantry, they were relatively useless against fortified
positions. Nor, he went on, were they so large or so invulner-
able as rumor had it; Zastros' elephants averaged between
twenty-two and twenty-six hands at the withers, not all of
them had tushes, and those that did seldom used the three- to

four-foot protuberances in fighting, rather lifting men and hurling them to earth with their serpentine noses or trampling them. The menace of fire set them wild, as did sudden loud noises.

Second, Portos knew he was not the only noble reduced to destitution by the long period of war. Those who still owned their lands would much rather be trying to bring them back to a state of productivity; instead, they were tramping across bare, burned fields and worrying about the welfare of any family they had left. Zastros' "regular" army was minuscule—perhaps a thousand men, perhaps less—and most of his huge, unwieldy host were privately-raised and -financed warbands. Few were armed or uniformed alike, they differed widely in habits and customs, and, though Zastros had had his staff group them into ten-thousand-man divisions having the proper proportions of cavalry and light infantry and pikemen, these arbitrary units seldom marched together, and if Zastros expected them to form battle lines together, he was the only one.

And, when Milo wondered aloud one day how he could keep the hotheaded and mutually hostile noblemen of Pitzburk and Harzburk from each other's throats until the battle was joined, Portos laughed until he was gasping.

"My High Lord, you have but two warbands at each other's throats. King Zastros is afflicted constantly with actual scores. That is how he became King, you know; it was not that the great *Thokeeksee* hated Zastros less, but that they hated one another more!"

When first he heard of the massacre of Martios and most of his pikemen, *Strahteegos Thoheeks* Glafkos went about his duties wearing a wide smile and few could recall ever having seen him so congenial. Then the accursed order had arrived from the High King, commanding him and what was left of his ten thousand to pursue the raiders and "avenge the murder of your brother, Martios."

Now, Glafkos had nothing against those raiders. He could only have wished that they had slain that sneak-thief bastard, Martios, considerably more slowly and painfully; further, had he ever even suspected that any degree of kinship existed betwixt him and the late *Vahrohnos*, he would have been strongly tempted to fall on his sword.

Nonetheless, since he *had* sworn his oaths to High King Zastros, he sent his squadron of cavalry out on a wide front to scout the raiders' trails, then broke camp and marched most of his light infantry and all of his archers toward the mountains. That night, at his marching-camp headquarters, the cavalry captain, his cousin, gave him the bad news: the three main passes, into which had led the trails of the raider columns, were blocked by rockslides. Weeks of work would be required to clear them and the workers would be constantly in danger from the cliffs on either side: however, certain of his scouts had found a couple of smaller passes that seemed to lead in the general direction, as well as a dry stream bed that was rough going for horses, but might serve for the passage of infantry.

Captain Vikos thrust out his dusty, booted legs, leaned back in his camp chair, and took a deep pull of his wine cup before continuing. "But, esteemed cousin, do not expect any advance to be cheap or easy, please. The scouts noted some cave mouths and a number of points that could be easily defended by a few good men. So if you do succeed in running the enemy to earth, you may well discover you have a treecat by the tail."

The chunky, graying *Strahteegos* cradled his cup in his big, square hands and nodded sagely. "Oh, I never dreamed that this little campaign would be a picnic, cousin. Personally, I think it's an asinine waste of time and men, but we settled on Zastros to replace King Chaos. If we *thoheeksee* don't obey him, who will?"

Vikos emptied his cup and sat up to refill it, then leaned back again, shrugging. "Well, cousin, this is as good a place to die as any, I suppose. If you decide to try all three ways at once, you'll have to proceed without cavalry on that stream bed."

"I'll be proceeding without cavalry, period," Glafkos bluntly informed him. "I know a little bit about fighting in mountains, as you may recall, cousin. Every warm body in my force will be going in afoot, officers, too. I'll be establishing a base camp midway between the two passes; your squadron will guard it. You'll also be responsible for keeping us supplied and for relaying any orders the High King sends. And keep a tight security on the camp, cousin. *Komees* Portos was no puling babe, yet his squadron was apparently wiped out, and you saw what passed with that devil-spawn. Martios."

"Never fear." The handsome Vikos smiled. "I'll have a care for my neck; but you have a care for yours, cousin. Don't forget, we're the last two men of our house."

"Yes, there's that, too." Glafkos slid a sealed oilskin pouch across to Vikos. "Should I not come out of those mountains, in the body, open that. It contains documents—all properly signed, witnessed, and sealed—assigning you my legal heir, with full claim to all my lands, cities, mines, and titles. As *Thoheeks*, you will of course take command of whatever these mountainmen leave of our warband. Should our High King refuse to confirm your military status, simply take the men and go back home; you swore oaths only to me, not him.

"Honestly, cousin, were it not for *my* oaths, I'd have been on the march south long since. I've a feeling that this entire venture is ill-starred. The army is far too large and the High King is draining the kingdom white to keep it supplied. Nor am I alone in my feelings, cousin. Many of my peers are of such mind, and if the High King meets with any major reverses or gets bogged down some way, there'll be more warbands marching south than north. Mark you my words."

The third day after their conversation, the first column returned, bearing with them the body of *Thoheeks* Glafkos, who—nearly fifty, and climbing a steep grade under a pitiless sun in half-armor—had suddenly dropped in his tracks, dead. Having no means of preserving the already decomposing body, nor wishing to inter his cousin's husk in foreign soil, Vikos had a pyre constructed and formally cremated the former commander.

Then he gathered the noble officers in his late cousin's pavilion and unsealed the pouch. With no hesitation, every officer took oaths to him, both civil and military. As these men were representative of the leading citizens of the duchy, this made Vikos *thoheeks*, in fact, requiring only the High King's approval of his military rank.

This, Zastros refused to do; citing Vikos' "youth" and "inexperience." He designated a soft-handed, foppish staff-officer the new commander of the division. It was at that moment that *Thoheeks* Vikos made his decision.

On the way back to the base camp, he stopped long enough to collect all of the men and animals Glafkos had left with the main army. At the base camp, where the badly mauled second column had at last returned, he called another officers' meeting and explained his intentions, offering to release the oaths of any who wished to remain in Karaleenos. There were no takers, so *Thoheeks* Vikos, his officers, and his men marched south the next morning.

At last, nearly three months after it crossed into Karaleenos, the vast hosts of the Southern Kingdom reached the south bank of the Luhmbuh River. Harrassment, disease, and desertion had cost them almost forty thousand warriors, but, including the camp followers, there were still nearly two hundred thousand souls in the string of encampments that soon were erected.

Milo ordered the horseclansmen and Tomos Gonsalos' cavalry back to the *castra*, though he left the Maklaud, a few picked mindspeakers, and all the cats in the mountains, where the great felines would be of far more service. The mountaineers and swampers were to maintain a steady pressure upon the vital supply lines, pick off scouts, small patrols, sentries, and stragglers, and conduct raids on Zastros' flanks and rear areas if conditions seemed favorable.

Ten feet south of the north bank, the bridge had been solidly blocked with a granite wall twelve feet high, and tapering in the rear from a six-foot base to a three-foot top. Just off the bridge, on either side of the road, were huge siege-engines, each capable of throwing an eighty-pound boulder the length of the bridge; and, atop the wall, were three engines casting six-foot spears with sufficient force to spit the biggest horse, end to end.

The High Lord had made good use of his time and resources. From above the western ford to the fringes of the eastern fens, along the northern bank of the river, small strong points of rammed earth and timber marked every half mile and each sheltered a handful of Horseclansmen and maiden-archers; additionally, the track above the floodline saw regular, heavily armed patrols. Well hidden in the secret waterways of the Luhmbuh's delta were thirty-seven biremes and nearly four thousand of Lord Alexandros' pirates.

Strahteegos Thoheeks Grahvos of Mehseepolis keh Eepseelospolis, *Vahrohnos* Mahvros of Lohfospolis, and *Vahrohnos* Neekos of Kehnooryospolis were spotted when their mounts first put hooves to the pinelog roadbed Milo had constructed over the old stones of the bridge. By the time they had completed their slow progress to the north, the High Lord and King Zenos were atop the wall to greet them.

They had come, announced Grahvos, to discuss the terms of Lord Milo's surrender. Milo courteously suggested that his pavilion might be a more comfortable setting for any discussions and, upon Grahvos' assent, several brawny troopers lowered a bosun chair and drew the three noblemen onto the wall.

Fresh mounts awaited them on the north bank. Then Milo and his guards led the emissaries on a wide swing, giving them a good look at the camps of well-armed, well-disciplined troops, at a horizon-long wagon train of supplies and at the bristling defenses of the *castra*.

When the three guests had been seated and wine had been served, Grahvos cleared his throat and asked bluntly, "How many men do Your Majesties command here?"

Milo chuckled. "You're a direct man, aren't you, Lord Grahvos? I'll be equally candid. I don't know, not exactly . . . though I can get the answer from my staff. In the camps you've seen and in some you haven't, I'd estimate a total fighting force in the neighborhood of one hundred thousand, perhaps a few thousand more."

"Then why," demanded the *Thoheeks*, "are Your Majesties' forces cowering behind walls and rivers? Why not meet us in open combat? True, we have a few more troops than you, overall, but you've the edge on us in cavalry."

Milo shrugged. "My reasons are my own, Lord Grahvos.

Suffice it to say that I have no intention of meeting in an open combat . . . not until I've bled you here for a while. You see, I have more troops arriving daily. How many reinforcements can your lord call up?"

Grahvos avoided the question. "Your Majesties, the High King has no desire for a battle himself. He has empowered me to speak for him in saying this: if Your Majesties will join forces with him, you may retain both your lands and your titles . . ."

"Be Zastros' lickspittle in my own kingdom?" interjected Zenos. "No, thank you, my lord!"

"Then we'll crush you." Grahvos sounded confident, but a brief scan of the man's surface thoughts showed Milo much confusion.

"Brave words," said the High Lord gravely. "Spoken by a man of proven bravery; but your position is untenable for long, Lord Grahvos . . . and I'm sure you know it.

"Your army has no boats, and you saw how solid is the wall blocking the bridge. We got those stones by destroying the only ford between here and the mountains. Of course, you could fell trees and try rafting. My catapult crews would be most gratified to see such an attempt . . . they'd also like to see an attempt to build a floating bridge, if you had that in mind.

"No, Lord Grahvos, your king sits at the end of a very long and most tenuous supply line, deep into hostile territory. His army has already suffered the loss of thousands by the activities of our partisans. Entire units have deserted and marched back to your homeland and, I understand, camp fever has incapacitated more thousands. It might occur to your king to send for his navy."

Grahvos started. That very thought had been on his mind.

Milo grated. "Forget that thought and persuade your king to do likewise. I had hulks towed from Kehnooryos Atheenahs and scuttled in the channel just west of the Luhmbuh delta. There is but the one channel and your dromonds could never negotiate it . . . now.

"The longer you sit on the south bank, Lord Grahvos, the higher will be your losses—more men and units will desert, more will be ambushed or killed in raids, more and more will die of disease. Any attempt to cross the river, by any of your available means, will be fatal to the troops employed."

And it was, to almost all of them.

The first . . . and last . . . assault was launched just after the next day's dawning. First onto the bridge came two elephants, sheathed from head to foot in huge plates of thick armor that turned the six-foot darts as though they had been blunt children's arrows. A sixty-pound boulder struck a massive headplate with a clang heard the length of the bridge, but the beast halted only long enough to trumpet his pain and displeasure, then came slowly on. It was then that Milo gave the order to fire the bridge.

The undersides of the logs making up the new roadbed had been thickly smeared with pitch and the interstices packed with tarred oakum and other inflammable substances and the first firearrow began a conflagration which, aided by a fortunate wind, was soon sweeping south, preceded by smoke from the green wood.

The elephants, scenting the oncoming danger, first tried to turn, then to back away only to be met by countless spear points. Finally, with the fire a bare five feet distant, the eastward elephant splintered the heavy rail and plunged into the river, sinking like a stone. Given room, the other spun about and plowed through the close-packed troops, leaving a wake of mangled flesh and crushed bone.

Miraculously, the east elephant came plodding out of the river onto the north bank, just downstream of the siege-engine emplacement. Milo tried to mindspeak the animal . . . and was mildly surprised when he succeeded.

After a short period of wordless mental soothing, he asked, "What are you called, sister?"

"You not . . . of my kind." It was half statement, half question.

Milo had had other experiences with animals that had never been mindspoken, and these guided him. Beckoning a couple of Horseclan mindspeakers, he gingerly approached the huge, dripping, mud-slimed beast. There was no longer a battle to require his supervision. The attackers were in full retreat before the fire . . . those who could walk, run, or

hobble; the rest were roasting on the bridge or drowning in
the river.

When the elephant saw them, she quickly rolled her trunk
out of harm's way, confused thoughts of battle-training flood-
ing the surface of her mind.

It was obvious that the headplates partially obscured her
vision, so Milo took pains to stand where she could clearly
see him, motioning the others to do the same. "Sister, we do
not wish to hurt you. Why do you wish to hurt us?"

He commenced the soothing again, this time joined by the
two clansmen. Gradually, the trunk uncurled, then sought
one of the sideplates and gently tugged at it. Her mindspeak
was plaintive. "Hurt. Take off?"

Endeavoring to exude far more confidence than he felt,
Milo paced deliberately to the cow's side and began unbuck-
ling the indicated plate. He started as he felt the finger-like
appendage at the end of her trunk touch him, but its touch
proved tender as a caress, wandering over his body, front and
back, head to toe. He was straining to reach the topmost
buckles when the truck closed about his waist and lifted him
high enough to reach them.

Seeing this cooperation, the two clansmen came up and began to help. A half hour saw the cow stripped of a quarter-
ton of plate and thick mail. Milo was at first appalled at her
condition—she seemed bare skin and bones, her ribs clearly
evident—and then he recalled that long, long supply line
winding through forageless countryside and constantly
menaced by his raiders; Zastros was having enough trouble
feeding his men, not to mention his animals.

He turned to one of his clansmen. "Rahdjuh, ride to the
castra and tell them to get any horses away from my pavilion. Captain Portos says our sister's kind afright horses; I'm
willing to take his word on the matter. Then ride on to the
quartermaster and tell Sub-Strahteegos Rahmos to send a
wagonload of his best hay and five or six bushels of cabbages to my pavilion immediately. Understand?"

"Yes, God-Milo." The clansman took off at a dead run
toward the picket line.

Milo turned back to the cow and rubbed a hand down the

rough, wrinkled trunk. She brought the trunk up, resting its end on his shoulder. "Sister, I wish to help you. I know that you need food, much food."

She again responded with the plaintive mindspeak. "Hungry . . . hungry many days. Good two-legs brother will give food?"

Milo beckoned the clansman to him and placed his arm across the smaller man's shoulders. "Sister, this is my brother, and he is good. He will take you to much food." He projected a mental picture of bales of fragrant hay and baskets of green-and-white cabbages.

The young clansman stood still while she subjected him to the same examination earlier afforded Milo, but he gasped when she suddenly grasped his torso, lifted him high off the ground, and sat him straddling the thick neck just behind the massive head. "Which way food?" she demanded.

Milo chuckled at the expression on the clansman's face. "Well, Gil, have you ever bestrode a bigger mount?"

Gil relaxed, grinned, and shook his head. "No, God-Milo, nor has any other Horseclansman, I think. She . . . and I . . . we are to go now to your pavilion?"

"Yes, Gil, and since she has accepted you, you are now her brother . . . and her keeper." He glanced at the blazon on the young man's cuirass, the broken saber and ferret head that proclaimed him a scion of Clan Djohnz. "Tell Chief Tchahrlee that you now have no other duties but to care for our sister here. Now, take her to the food; those bastards over there have been starving her."

The night after the abortive assault, a score of biremes crept upriver, their oars muffled. Avoiding the larger camp of Zastros, they staged four almost simultaneous attacks on as many camps, while a force of swampers struck the easternmost camp and a strong contingent of mounted irregulars brought fire and sword to the rear areas. The swampers, unaccustomed to fighting in the open, took heavy losses, but the casualties of the pirates and the mountaineers were minimal. The swampers did not attack again, but the reavers and the mountainmen did, three more nights in a row, never striking the same camps.

The scattered encampments began to move closer, one to the next, until most of the still-tremendous force was concentrated in the low, swampy area just south of the bridge. And, of course, the fevers ran rampant.

Supplies were dropping perilously low, for few trains were intact when they arrived . . . if they arrived. And they all told tales of running fights and ambuscades, of roadsides littered with skeletons and rotting flesh and charred wagons. So High King Zastros sent south an order for a huge train; to guard the train, he dispatched four squadrons of cavalry. What remained of the train eventually trickled in; the last they had seen of the five thousand cavalry, the horsemen were splitting into small groups and heading for home.

12

———••◆••———

Lillian Landor opened her dark-blue eyes and stretched her white arms luxuriously, then swung her shapely legs over the edge of the low couch and sat up. On the other side of the couch, High King Zastros lay like a log, only the movement of his chest denoting that there was life in the hairy body.

The black-haired woman made use of the silver chamber-pot, then padded across the thickly carpeted floor of the lamp-lit, silk-walled room. Taking a position in the middle of the room where the ceiling was higher, she went through ten minutes of intricate exercises to loosen long unused muscles.

God! she thought. God, it's good to be back in a youthful, limber body, again.

She looked with loathing upon the body of Zastros, deep in drugged slumber on the couch. His every major bone and joint must have been broken or sprained seriously at least once in his lifetime, not to mention the countless scars of cuts, slashes, stabs, and thrusts; occupancy of such a body, especially in rainy weather, was endless, dull agony.

Perspiring lightly from her exertions, she went to the wash-stand, filled the basin, and began to sponge her resilient, ala-baster skin, while regarding her heart-shaped face in a mirror of polished steel. Briefly closing her eyes, she tried to recall what her own face—the face of the body in which she had been born seven hundred years before—had looked like.

Nodding, she murmured to herself, "It was dark-haired too . . . I think. Christ, it's so damned hard to remember when you've had a couple of dozen bodies since then . . . no, more

133

than that, thirty, anyway, maybe more. Sometimes I feel like a goddamned vampire. If we could only take one of those mutants apart, find out what causative factors are responsible for their regeneration. If I could think of a way to get my hands on this Milo . . . hmmm."

Musing, she drew a robe over her bare skin and passed into the outer room to kneel before one of a pair of "ornamental" chests. Placing both her delicate hands atop the lid, she spread her fingers and pressed their tips upon eight metal studs in an intricate sequence.

Earlier that evening, a small boat had grounded at a well-hidden spot on the south bank and a heavily cloaked man had stepped ashore, mounted a waiting horse and spurred off into the darkness.

At the fringe of the main camp, *Strahteegos* Grahvos' most trusted retainers stood guard about his pavilion, their bared steel turning away any who came near. When a horseman, both his face and body muffled in a dark cloak, rode up, he leaned from his saddle, whispered a few words to an officer, and was immediately passed through.

Within the main room of the pavilion, Grahvos and seven other *thoheeksee* conversed in low, guarded tones. When a ninth man entered, Grahvos hurried over to him and they exchanged a few whispered sentences. Then the newcomer laid aside his cloak and accompanied the old *Strahteegos* back to the table.

Grahvos tapped his knuckles on the table and the other nobles broke off their conversations to turn toward him. "Gentlemen, I declare the Council of *Thoheeksee* . . . what's now left of us, at least . . . now in session. I think that most of you know Captain *Vahrohnos* Mahvros of Lohfospolis. It was he who had the courage to undertake the mission of which I spoke earlier. He has just returned from the camp of High Lord Milo and King Zenos, where he spoke in my name. He . . . but let him tell of it." He sat down.

Mahvros looked half again his thirty years. His darkly handsome face was drawn with fatigue and the nervous strain of the last day. But his voice was strong. "My lords, I spent most of the afternoon and early evening with High Lord

Milo, King Zenos of Karaleenos, Lord Alexandros of the Sea Isles and *Thoheeks* Djefree of Kumbuhluhn, though the High Lord seemed to speak for all most of the time.

"He swears that no man or body of men marching south will be harmed or hindered; indeed, if they march along the main traderoad, they can be certain of guides to show them to unpolluted water.

"The High Lord emphasized that he wants none of our arms or supplies or equipment. We are welcome to bear back anything we brought north. He demands only the surrender of the persons of the High King and the Queen."

"Haarumph!" Thoheeks Mahnos of Ehpohtispolis interjected. "He is most welcome to that pair, say I. Good riddance to bad rubbish!"

"Yes, yes," Grahvos agreed. "We made a serious mistake with Zastros, but none of us could have known at the time how much he had changed in his three years of exile. We now know and, hopefully, it's not too late to save our homelands from any more of his misrule."

Another voice entered the conversation—the gritty bass of *Thoheeks* Bahos growled. "I went along with the majority— every man here knows that—but I told you then that Zastros was not Zastros. Our fathers' duchies adjoined. I've known the man all his life, and the Zastros of the last year is *not* the Zastros of years agone!"

"Well, be that as it may be," Grahvos snapped. "The High Lord Milo wants the High King and his witch-wife. Our alternatives are few: we can continue to sit here, while the men desert individually and in whole units, until starvation, or camp fever or an arrow in the night takes us; or we can try another assault on that goddamned deathtrap of a bridge . . . though, to my way of thinking, falling on our swords would be an easier way of suiciding.

"I say that we leave Zastros and his wife to our esteemed former foes and take our men back home; God knows, we and they have enough to do there. How says the Council?"

Seven ayes answered.

"Now that that is settled," Grahvos went hurriedly on, "let's bring another thorny matter into the open. Who *is* going to rule without Zastros? Each of us has as much claim to

the Dragon Throne as the next. But can the Southern Kingdom survive another three or more years of civil war and anarchy? I think not.

"Look around this table, gentlemen. Our Council was once
made up of two and thirty *thoheeksee*; including Zastros,
there are now but nine in our camp. If young Vikos made it
back safely, there are two, living *thoheeksee* in all of the
Southern Kingdom, and the late King probably died by his
own hand.

"What of the rest, gentlemen? Twenty *thoheeksee*, almost
two-thirds of the original Council, died senselessly and use-
lessly while fighting like curs over a stinking piece of offal!

"I say: no more, gentlemen, no more! If we name another
of our own number king, how long will it be before one or
more of us is tempted to overthrow him, replace him, eh?"

There were sober nods and mutterings of agreement
around the table.

At length, *Thoheeks* Bahos grunted the obvious question.
"Then what are we to do, Grahvos? Our kingdom *must* have
a strong ruler, but a tyrant like Hyamos and his lousy son
will beget another rebellion."

"The High Lord Milo of Kehnooryos Ehlahs, Karaleenos
keh Kuhmbuhlun has freely offered the thirty-three duchies
of the Southern Kingdom full-standing memberships in his
Confederation. All nobles will retain their lands, cities, rights,
and titles; only their sworn allegiance will change. We will
have *no* king; each *thoheeks* will act as royal governor of his
duchy for the High Lord. The High Lord or his emissary will
meet with the full Council each year to work out taxes and
any other business matters."

The first to speak after Grahvos had dropped his bombshell
was Mahnos. "What of our warbands?"

"We will, of course, be expected to furnish men for the
Army of the Confederation, and to see to the training of the
spear levy. Nor will noblemen be denied bodyguards and
armed retainers, but the large warbands are to be dissolved."

Mahnos nodded emphatically. "Good and good again. Give
a man a small army to play with and all hell breaks loose.
Besides, I'd rather see my people pushing plows than pikes.
You have my 'aye,' Grahvos."

Within a scant hour it was settled, for the firm yet fair government of Kehnooryos Ehlahs had been the subject of speculation and admiration for the thirty years 'since its inception; and all the *thoheeksee* agreed that almost any form of rule was preferable to the last few years. The meeting broke up and they scattered to their various commands to order their forces, agreeing to meet, each with retinues of reliable, well-armed men, at Zastros' pavilion at a specified time.

Lillian leisurely set up the transceiver, attaching it to the powerpack in the matching chest and to its antenna—that long, slender brass rod that she, while in Zastros' body, had had permanently affixed to the highest point of the pavilion. Then she plugged in the mike and carefully adjusted the frequency. There was, she knew, no chance of discovery or interruption this time, for Zastros was heavily sedated—even were he not, only the timbre of her voice and those words known to no other could bring him out of his trance-state. Nor were the guards to be expected to check this far into the pavilion until they changed, and that was at least two hours away.

She depressed the button that gave out her call signal. Almost immediately a man's voice crackled from the set.

"This is the J. & R. Kennedy Center. Who's calling, please?"

"Dr. Landor. This is Dr. Lillian Landor. Who is the board member on duty tonight?"

"Uhhh, Dr. Crawley, ma'am. You wish to speak with him?"

"Of course I want to speak with him, you dunce! Why else do you think I called? And, wait a minute!" she snapped. 'I hold four degrees buster. I've as much right to the title 'Doctor' as has any other board member. If I hear one more goddamned *ma'am* out of you, you'll spend the next ten years in the body of a goddamned alligator! You get me, you goddamned chauvinist?"

The man stammered some unintelligible reply. Then there was dead air for a short while while she fidgeted and silently fumed.

A new voice came through the speaker. "This is Bud Crawley, Lily. What seems to be the problem this time?"

"Dr. Crawley," she replied icily, "I warned you all about the riskiness of this insanity from the start, and I knew I was right, even if you didn't. Well, the army is at the Little Pee Dee River, just west of the ocean swamps, and it cannot go any farther north, not without help from the Center."

"What kind of help, Lily?" Crawley sounded wary.

"We have no boats to cross the river and, even if we did, they'd never make it in the face of catapults and horse-archers and God knows how many boatloads of pirates from those damned islands where Bermuda used to be. The bridge we'd expected to use has had a goddamned wall built right across it. I ordered it overrun, but these goddamned cowards lost so many men on the first assault that the second and third waves flatly refused to attack.

"They're dying like flies and deserting in droves and I know it's just a matter of time before they murder Zastros and call the whole thing off, if they can patch together some kind of deal with that goddamned mutant bastard. So I want out, *now!* Send a copter for me or send me help, one of the two."

"Hmmm," replied Crawley. "Hang on, Lily. I'll have to check the map with someone who knows more about transportation than I do."

A third male voice addressed her. "Doctor, this is O'Hare, transportation. Can you read me the coordinates off your transceiver? Those dials are located . . ."

"Goddamn it, *I* know where they're located!" she snarled into the mike. "Do you think I'm stupid?"

"N . . . no, ma'am," he stuttered.

"If you goddamned bastards don't stop calling me ma'am . . ." Her infuriated voice had risen to almost a shout and she broke off short. The last thing she wanted in here right now was a guard. "The coordinates are: thirty-five degrees and twenty-eight minutes latitude, seventy-nine degrees and two minutes longitude."

After a moment O'Hare said: "Well, ma' . . . uh, Dr. Landor, you're not on the little Pee Dee, you're on the *Lumber River!*"

"Well, ma' . . . uh, *Mr.* O'Hare," she scathingly mimicked him, "what the hell difference does it make?"

Crawley's voice cut in gravely. "Quite a bit, actually, Lily. You see, where you are now is beyond the range of any of our copters. We can neither get help to you *nor* pick you up, I'm afraid."

"Goddamn your ass, Bud Crawley! What kind of crap are you trying to feed me?" Lillian spluttered furiously. "*I* happen to *know* that the big copters have a range of five hundred miles. I'm not *that* far from the Center, and don't try to tell me I am, you son-of-a-bitch, you! The distance dial on this goddamned transceiver reads: 742.5 kilometers."

"Actually, 742.531," Crawley announced dryly. "Roughly 461.5 miles, Lily. And, yes, the maximum range of the large copters *is* five hundred miles, but that is a *round-trip* figure. Yes, we could get one up to you, but it couldn't get back. Don't you see?"

"Well, what the hell, Crawley, let them come up and blow that damned wall off the bridge and scatter the mutant's army. Then they can march with me."

Crawley sighed. "Lily, Lily, you know as well as do I what the board would say to that. We cannot—have not the facilities to—replace copters and there are no refueling points that far north."

Lillian was almost shouting again. "Why can't the five-thumbed bastards bring their extra goddamned fuel with them. I can remember that planes used to do it."

She could hear O'Hare's voice in the background as Crawley briefly conferred with him. Then, "I'm most sorry, Lily, but that idea is just not practical. You see, the extra weight of the fuel would decrease the overall range. I'm afraid you're just caught in quite a vicious circle, old girl."

"Don't 'old girl' me, you damned Limey fairy!" she hissed. "Just tell me how you're going to get me out of this frigging mess your goddamned masculine stupidity got me into!"

His voice cooled noticeably. "I'm looking at the map now, Dr. Lander. Lieutenant O'Hare assures me that, if you can get even as far west and south as thirty-degrees no minutes latitude, eighty-two degrees thirty minutes longitude, we shall have no difficulty succoring you."

"Even if I can find a way to get out of this camp and down to whatever that is, how in the hell am I going to know it? Grid lines aren't painted on the goddamned grass, you know; and how the hell am I going to let you know I got there, you pigs?"

"Your transceiver will . . ." began Crawley.

"Screw a goddamned transceiver and screw you, too!" She made no more efforts to muffle her voice. "How am I supposed to carry the damned thing, Crawley, on my goddamned back? Altogether, these two units must weigh three hundred pounds!"

"Three hundred forty-two and three-quarters," amended Crawley. "A modest load for a good pack mule or horse, I should think."

"Crawley, I know you're about as dense as the day is long, you mammy jammer! How many times do I have to tell you? It's a matter of time, a short time in all likelihood, until some of these goddamned Greeks come in here and murder Zastros, so I can't get out of camp in *his* body, they'd never let it out alive, and I'd never be allowed to leave without him . . . much less find somebody to find and saddle and load a goddamned packhorse for me." She ran out of breath, took several deep ones, and regained a measure of composure. "Crawley, I just might be able to steal one horse and get out of here alone. But how can a young woman traveling alone get back to one of our outposts?"

"As I remember, Lily, your present body is quite attractive, though a wee bit too slender for my own tastes. Nonetheless, you should have no trouble getting back. Just find a strong or wealthy man and . . . be nice to him." He paused, then went on, unable to entirely mask his merriment. "Who knows, Lily, after all these centuries you might decide you like it."

"You . . . you . . . you no-good, dirty-minded sexist animal!" she screamed. "You and your kind, you'd just *love* to know I made the trip on my goddamned back so you could have something to snicker about. When you look at a woman, none of you bastards ever even thinks that her mind might be as good or better than yours; no, all that you can think about is using her body for your own selfish . . ."

She broke off suddenly, startled by a noise in the anteroom. Then the mike slipped from her hand as a spearman of Zastros' bodyguard entered.

At that moment, Crawley inquired, "Lily! Lily! Dr. Landor! Can you hear my transmission?"

Making the ages-old hand sign against evil, the wide-eyed guard backed toward the anteroom, half whimpering, "*Witch! Witchcraft!*"

Fully aware of her danger, Lillian arose, smiling and extending a hand to the terrified soldier. "Oh, Solvos, you know I'm no witch. This chest is simply a toy with which I amuse myself while my dear lord sleeps. Here, give me your hand and look into my eyes."

But he comprehended no single word she spoke, except for his own name. In her confusion, she was still talking in twentieth-century American English—as different from Old Merikan as the language of Chaucer. He only knew that she *was* speaking and using his name and advancing at him, and he suspected an attempt to ensorcell him. Just before he turned to run, he lashed out at her with the ferrule of his spear. He felt it strike, then took off as if Satan himself were hard on his heels.

Without the High King's pavilion, *Strahteegos* Grahvos could make neither heads nor tails of the white-faced, stuttering spearman's words. Knocking the heavy, solid-brass dress spear from his hand, Grahvos took the man's shoulders and shook him violently. Even then, all that he could understand of the confused utterings were repeated references to witches, witchcraft, spells, and men imprisoned in magical chests. Disgustedly, he threw the soldier aside and strode purposefully toward the entry, the other nobles crowding behind him.

A limp hand extended into the anteroom. Grahvos carefully pulled aside the curtains to disclose the crumpled form of Lady Lilyuhn, still swathed in her robe of brocade silk. But the crackling radio set drew his attention. He stepped over her and crossed to squat in front of it. All at once, the crackling ceased and Crawley's voice impatiently demanded, "Blast you, Lily, stop playing games! I know your transceiver's still on. Acknowledge my transmission. Damn it, Charley, are you certain this is the proper frequency?"

The front rank of nobles went as wide-eyed and ashen as had the spearman. Grahvos looked up in time to see *Thoheeks* Mahnos rapidly crossing himself, his lips moving in half-forgotten prayers.

"Oh, for the love of God, Mahnos," Grahvos expostulated, "grow up! This is some sophisticated variety of machine, nothing more."

He picked up the mike lying on the carpet and examined it carefully. "This is wrought of that odd material the Elder People employed . . . *plahsteek*, I think it was called. The machine might even be from those times."

Though frightened, like all humans, of those things they did not understand, the nobles were not cowards. Seeing Grahvos unharmed, they slowly entered the inner chamber and scrutinized the strange device, first from a distance, then closer. But no more voices came from it, only a low-pitched hum and sporadic crackling sounds.

While they gaped at this wonder and gradually overcame their fears, far to the south, in the midst of the Great Southern Swamp, Dr. Bud Crawley was speaking into an intercom.

"Sir, I am afraid that we must write off Dr. Landor and the project to which she was assigned." Briefly, deleting her expletives and verbal abuse, he quoted Lillian's last report, closing by saying, "Then she suddenly broke off in the middle of a sentence, although she failed to deactivate the transceiver. There were some muffled noises, then several minutes of silence. The next voices I could hear distinctly were all masculine and all were speaking Greek."

The senior director's voice sounded sleepy. "All right, Bud, and thank you. Apparently Dr. Landor allowed herself more time than she really had. It was possibly our mistake to assign her to such a mission, anyway; she hated men—all men—and the emotion of hate tends to cloud one's judgment and perceptiveness as much as does the emotion of love. We must exercise more care in the future; there're too few of us to waste.

"But, nonetheless, Bud, you might try leaving our transceiver on that frequency for a while. Miracles happen, you know. She might be in hiding."

Lillian was in hiding. When the spear butt had crashed

against her body's delicate skull, there had been a moment of shocked confusion; then she had felt the life-force leaving her body. Frantically, unthinkingly, she re-entered Zastros. Only when the transference was complete did she think what this meant. True, the drugs would wear off in time, but his body would never achieve full consciousness or the ability to move and speak without . . . without those few, simple words. But those words must be spoken through the mouth and vocal apparatus of that beautiful young body that lay almost dead on the floor of the dressing chamber. And she realized that she was not hiding safely—she was *trapped!*

Willing Zastros' recumbent body to its maximum possible awareness, she heard the nobles enter the pavilion, heard that ass, Crawley, accuse her—a responsible, mature woman with no less than *four* degrees—of "playing games." The nobles milled about the dressing chamber for a short while, exclaiming over various aspects of the radio.

Children! Lillian thought contemptuously. But, then, all men are basically dirty-minded little boys!

She heard the clump of boots and the clank of armor as someone came toward the couch, and she strove vainly to force Zastros' eyelids to open. Then a rough hand had taken the inert body's arm and shaken it vigorously.

A voice she recognized as that of *Strahteegos* Grahvos spoke harshly. "Zastros! Zastros! Damn your eyes, Zastros, wake up!" The hand let go and the boots clumped back. "He's out like a snuffed torch, gentlemen."

Someone muttered something Zastros' ears could not pick up the meaning of.

"How many times do I have to tell you to stop that foolishness!" barked Grahvos' voice. "Sorcery, my calloused butt! Wine or drugs did this, probably both together; we all know he kept his wife drugged most of the time, so he obviously uses them, too.

"But it doesn't matter; awake or asleep, he's still deposed. Let High Lord Milo waken him. We came mainly for the jewels and the gold. Let's find them and get on the march. One of you pull off this house signet and find his sword. They should go to his nephew, Kathros. But no obvious plundering, gentlemen; if you must steal, steal small. I don't want our prospective overlord to think ill of us, nor should you; remember, our future lies with his Confederation."

After a brief period of pushing about of furniture, dragging and clattering noises, and a short, sharp pain in Zastros' right thumb as his signet was jerked off, Lillian heard the men's voices fade away into the distance, leaving her alone in her refuge-become-prison. She made a stab at re-entering the body in the other room, but the way was closed, and no amount of will could budge so much as the tiniest muscle of Zastros' hulk.

There was a short, deadly battle with the former High King's bodyguard officers when the nobles bore the royal treasures from the pavilion and made to load them onto a waiting wagon, but the retainers of the *thoheeksee* ruthlessly cut down any who drew sword or lowered spear against them. With the officers all dead or dying, the rest of the guard wisely slipped away, tearing off their Green Dragon tabards as they went—naught could be gained in the support of a deposed and probably dead king.

Grahvos, well aware that whatever was left would certainly be looted by the unattached camp followers, stationed two hundred heavy infantry under command of *Vahrohnos* Mahvros to guard the ex-King's pavilion and its environs until the High Lord's troops arrived. He also entrusted to the younger man a large package of documents—written oaths of fealty to the Confederation—all signed, witnessed, and sealed, from every landholder in the dispersing army.

A full day and then another night had been required to prepare the warbands for the retrograde movement. By the thirty-sixth hour after the nobles had looted Zastros' treasures, the Green Dragon banner atop his pavilion waved over a scene of desolation. Outside the royal enclosure, precious few tents remained. Only discarded or broken equipment was left and a horde of human scavengers flitted through swarms of flies feasting on latrines and garbage pits.

Thoheeks Grahvos was the last to depart, having seen most of the troops on the march before dawn. Leaving his personal detachment at the foot of the hill, he rode up to the royal enclosure and dismounted before the pavilion.

"Any trouble so far, Mahvros?"

The young nobleman shook his head. "Nor do I expect any, my lord. Oh, my boys had to crack a couple of heads before we convinced the scum that we meant business, but we've been avoided since then."

"And when the rest of us are on the road?" asked the *Thoheeks* skeptically.

"There're damned few soldiers down there, my lord. And none of the skulkers are organized—it's every man for himself. No, everything will be as it is when the Confederation troops get here." Mahvros smiled.

Grahvos asked, "What of Zastros? Has he awakened yet?"

"No, my lord, he lives, but still he sleeps," replied the *Vahrohnos*, adding, "but we had to bury the Lady Lilyuhn. She was beginning to stink."

Grahvos shrugged. "It couldn't be helped. That guard probably killed her. There was fresh blood on his spear butt. But tell the High Lord that I'm sorry.

"Also, Mahvros, tell him that I'll see that the Thirty-three convene in the capital whenever he desires. I am certain that he and King Zenos will want some form of reparations, but emphasize, please, that some few years will be necessary to put our demesnes back on a paying basis."

He put foot to stirrup, then turned back. "One other thing, Mahvros, my boy; the Council met for a short session this morning. *Thoheeks* Pahlios was your overlord, was he not?"

"Yes, my lord, but he was slain nearly three years ago. I . . ."

"Just so," Grahvos interrupted. "He and all his male kin in the one battle. We're going to have to affirm or choose the remainder of the Thirty-three rather quickly, and we want men we know will support us and the Confederation. That's why we chose you to succeed the late Pahlios."

Delving into his right boot-top, Grahvos brought out a slender roll of parchment. "Guard this well, *Thoheeks* Mahvros. When you're back, ride to the capital and the Council will loan you troops enough to secure your new lands.

"Now, I must be gone." He mounted and, from his saddle,

extended his hand. "May God bless and keep you, lad, and may He bring you safely home."

Reining about, he trotted out of the compound and down the hill.

13

It was almost a week before Milo made it across the river. The wall had to be dismantled, of course, but that alone would not have detained him, for Lord Alexandros had left a couple of biremes and crews for his use. However, when certain of the Middle Kingdoms' nobles were apprised that there would be no battle, after all, they split into two factions at the cores of which were the contingents from Harzburk and Pitzburk. Armed to the teeth, the factions mounted and rode into the fields west of the camp. And the resulting melée was only the first and largest. It was a very hectic period for the High Lord.

At length, he had all the northern troops and their battered nobles on the march, their units separated and shepherded by strong bodies of Confederation regulars and Confederation-contracted Freefighters.

Dressed in his best clothing and finest armor, Milo strode out of his pavilion and had already ordered a charger when he felt a familiar touch on the back of his neck. Behind him stood the elephant.

Sunshine—she had chosen the name herself as her mind-speak improved with usage—was noticeably sleeker, as she well should have been, thought Milo, considering the fantastic amounts of food she had consumed. From all over the camp, men had come not just to see her, but to watch her eat. And "hungry as the elephant" had become a common expression to Milo's army.

When Milo turned, Sunshine moved closer and placed her

trunk tip on his shoulder so that its appendage might caress his skin. "Please God-Milo," she begged, "do not send Sunshine away from you today. Take her with you."

"Sunshine," Milo gently and patiently mindspoke, "we have been through all this before. Where I live is cold for much of the year, colder than the land from which you came. You would quickly die there. You *must* go back south, Sunshine, but Gil will be with you all the way. He will see that you eat all you want and that no man harms you. And when I come to your land, I will visit you. Will not that make Sunshine happy?"

Her answer surprised him. "Let Sunshine bear God-Milo across the river, then, please. You will ride safer on Sunshine than on that skinny-legged little creature." She pointed her trunk at where Milo's groom stood waiting with a seventeen-hand war horse. "If you fight, how can *that* one protect you? Sunshine has slain many two-legs."

"There will be no fight, Sunshine," Milo assured her. "Those who were my enemies are now my friends, and you must promise not to hurt the few of them who remain beyond the river; you and Gil will be traveling with them."

"Sunshine will not hurt any creatures Gil does not tell her to hurt," she spoke. Then, "But . . . please ride Sunshine . . . ?"

"Why, Sunshine," Milo asked, "is it so important to you that you carry me across the bridge?"

Sunshine came closer, tenderly wrapping him about with her trunk. "God-Milo is the first two-leg who was ever good to Sunshine, who spoke to her and treated her like . . . like a two-leg. Sunshine cannot stay with God-Milo to serve him all her days, as she should. Will not God-Milo allow her to serve him *once* . . . ?"

What the hell, thought Milo, how much more impressive an appearance could I make than arriving on an elephant?

"Gil!" he farspoke. "Have you rigged any sort of saddle for Sunshine?"

Gil stepped from behind the elephant, a sheepish grin on his face and his arms filled with an altered saddle and an assortment of odd harness.

"Damn it!" exclaimed Milo aloud. "You two *planned* this in advance! Admit it, kinsman!"

"Yes, God-Milo, Sunshine and I planned," Gil mindspoke. "But, God-Milo, she is very grateful to you . . . and she loves you. Often has our Clanbard said that nothing is so unkind as to force a man or woman to swallow honest gratitude unexpressed."

Milo mindcalled the groom and the three of them saddled Sunshine. The saddle perfectly fitted the area just behind her head.

That done, Milo addressed Gil. "All right, you ride my charger and get a pack animal for your gear." He turned back to his huge mount. "Very well, my dear, you may help me aboard."

"So the guard," *Thoheeks* Mahvros continued, "hearing her shout in some unknown tongue, came into the tent and found her crouching before this device. Exactly what happened then, no one knows, not even the guard, who can only say that he fended her off with the butt of his spear, then ran. He thought her a witch, you see."

"And he may not have been too far off the mark," thought Milo. "Not if she was what I suspect."

"When Lord Grahvos and I and the rest came in, she was stretched on the floor here." Mahvros indicated a spot on the carpet, stiff and crusty with dried blood. "The left side of her skull was cracked, just above and behind the ear, and she no longer was breathing.

"The device spoke in a man's voice, but none of us could understand the words, though some later said they thought to have once heard a similar language. No one could recall where or when or what it was called. The voice but spoke a short time, then Lord Grahvos examined it and persuaded others of us to do so. It made various noises for a while. Then suddenly they ended and it has not been touched since."

Milo squatted before the odd chest and lifted the mike, then studied the various dials and knobs and switches adorning the exposed face. Turning to King Zenos, *Thoheeks* Grimnos, and the rest, he said, "This, gentlemen, is what the people who lived seven hundred years ago called a 'radio.' It was used to transmit spoken messages long distances. There is

nothing of witchcraft about it, although I think that the pur-
poses of the men and women who constructed this one and
used it are as sinister as any wizard and warlock who ever
took breath."

A closer examination revealed why the noises had so suddenly ceased. The cord that had been connected to a second
chest had been somehow disconnected. Milo reconnected it
and the resultant spark brought starts to the other men. As
the instrument warmed up, it first emitted a low hum, then a
faint static.

"Is anyone receiving my transmission?" Milo spoke into
the mike. He said it again, then grinned ruefully and
switched from Ehleenokos to what he hoped, after all these
years, was twentieth-century American usage.

There was a louder crackling, then a voice answered in the
same language. "Yes, your transmission is being received.
Who are you? Where is Lily . . . uh, Dr. Lillian Landor?"

"If you mean the woman who last used this radio, she's
dead," answered Milo shortly. "As for me, I'm Milo Morai,
High Lord of Kehnooryos Ehlahs. With whom am I speaking?"

The voice became agitated. "You . . . you're the *mutant*,
the one who's lived in a single body since the war?"

"Okay, you know who *I* am!" snapped Milo. "Now, who
the hell are you?"

But a second voice cut in to answer him, a smooth, polished, unruffled voice. "Mr. Morai, I am Dr. Sternheimer, the
Senior Director of the J. & R. Kennedy Memorial Center.
We would very much like to meet with you, at your convenience, of course. We can pick you up and fly you down
from anywhere within a two-hundred mile radius of the Center."

Milo's laugh was harsh and humorless. "Oh, yes, I'll just
bet you types would very much like to get your claws into
me. And I can imagine why, too! So you can dig out of my
flesh whatever it is that makes us more or less immortal. No,
thank you, Dr. Sternheimer. I don't care to be the subject in
a vivisection!"

"Please, wait, you don't understand, Mr. Morai . . ."
Sternheimer began.

But Milo cut him off. "No, I don't understand, Doctor; I

don't understand why you creeps continue to embroil yourselves in the affairs of the Ehleens. What can you hope to gain? Are you running low on bodies?"

He was answered with a question. "Mr. Morai, are you an American citizen?"

"I *was*," replied Milo. "But what has that to do with my previous question, Doctor?"

Sternheimer's tones became fervid. "We, Mr. Morai, are attempting to re-establish *The United States of America!*"

This time Milo's laughter was real. "Doctor, if you're not pulling my leg, I advise you to have a long chat with one of your shrinks. Have you lost track of time? Doctor, this is, I believe, the twenty-seventh century A.D. The United States, as you and I knew it, has been dead a long time. Why not let it rest in peace?"

"Because, Mr. Morai, *I* am a patriot!" announced Sternheimer.

Milo laughed again. "So patriotic are you—or were you— that you disregarded the orders of the Congress and your superiors in H.E.W. to discontinue your vampiric experiments and destroy all notes and records of them."

"But I *knew* that our work was terribly important, Mr. Morai, and events bear out my belief!" Sternheimer exclaimed. "Besides, who were those damned, ignorant politicians to dictate to *me*?"

"They were the elected congressmen of the citizens whose taxes paid for your experiments, Doctor," said Milo coolly.

This time, it was Sternheimer who expelled a snort of hard laughter. "The Great Unwashed Masses? Oh, come now, Mr. Morai, you know as well as I do that those congressional fools simply overreacted to a few letters from religious fanatics and the tripe churned out by a handful of newsmongering simpletons calling themselves 'journalists'! When *we* re-establish our nation, there will be no such aggregation of august fools. The people will be governed sensibly, scientifically."

"Forget it, Sternheimer." Milo's voice was become glacial. "I remind you again; this is not the world we knew, long ago. Today's people need you and your plans of a scientific dictatorship as much as they need a hole in the head. And I serve you fair warning: keep your damned vampires out of my lands—which now include the Southern Kingdom as well as Karaleenos and Kehnooryos Ehlahs, incidentally. I'll scotch every one of your people I can lay my hands on, Sternheimer, and don't you forget it!"

Sternheimer abruptly turned on the charm once more. "My dear Mr. Morai, you do misunderstand. How I wish we could speak face to face, man to man, so that I might convince you of . . ."

"Sternheimer, you couldn't convince me that dung stinks! So don't waste your breath trying psychology on me. Just remember what I said, what I promised to do to any of your parasites I catch, and keep them out of my Confederation. I expect I'll have my work cut out for me during the next couple of centuries, and I'll have no mercy on any of your ghouls who traipse about stirring things up." Milo hurled the mike to the floor.

"Wait a minute, Mr. Morai." Sternheimer's next words remained unheard, for Milo spun the frequency knob, losing the nasal voice in a welter of static.

The High Lord disconnected the power source, then ordered his guards that the two chests be carried to the center of the bridge and dumped into the river.

Nothing that was done to Zastros' body could evoke even the fluttering of an eyelid—shaking him did no good, nor did slaps or blows or dagger points pushed into the most sensitive spots on his body, not even torch flames applied to his fingertips and toes.

"And he has been just so, Lord Milo, since the night we came to depose him," asserted Mahvros. "He swallows liquids if we open his jaws and dribble them into his mouth, but he cannot eat."

Milo gazed down on the inert body, now bruised and burned and bleeding. He attempted to enter the mind, but he found it shielded. He then surmised the actual fact, though he never knew it for such.

"Gentlemen, I imagine that Zastros' wife, who was the agent of a very evil man far south of here, drugged her husband. She probably wished him unconscious while she used that radio to contact her lord. We'll never know the antidote that might restore him to consciousness until we know what drugs she used, and she took that knowledge with her to her grave. His body would starve to death ere we might chance upon that antidote. The kindest thing to do now is to grant him a clean, quick death."

So saying, he drew his dirk.

Lillian heard it all, heard both sides of the mutant's conversation with the Senior Director, heard the order to destroy her transceiver—her only possible link with the Center—heard all their attempts to arouse Zastros' body; though she felt each and every excruciating agony and screamed almost incessantly, no single sound emerged from the body's lips. Then she heard Milo's last words, heard his weapon snick from its case.

She felt fingertips move on the chest, locate the spot and lift away, to be replaced by the knife point. Then she was silently screaming out the unbearable anguish of the cold, sharp blade entering the body's heart; unmoving, she writhed in pain as he jerked the double-edged weapon, slicing the organ to speed death.

Frantically, Lillian cast about, seeking a sleeping or unconscious body—any body, human or otherwise—fruitlessly. Faintly, she heard voices and the clumping of heavy boots. Then there was silence.

Thus, did Dr. Lillian Landor (holder of *four* degrees), who had hated all male humans for most of the seven hundred years of her life, at last meet death . . . in a man's body.

14

Early in that month called *Thekembrios*, Milo and Mara lay reclined upon a mound of cushions, sipping cordials and gazing into the heart of a crackling, popping wood fire. The evening had been one of those rare occasions on which they had been able to dine alone, in their suite, and the remains of the meal littered a table nearby.

He tried to enter her mind, failed, and said aloud, "What are you thinking of that you must shield your thoughts."

She smiled ruefully. "Sorry, Milo. We must shield our thoughts so much of our days, you know. But I didn't mean to shut you out.

"No, I was thinking of you . . . in a way. I was thinking of the first winter I spent with you in that damned drafty tent at Ehlai. God, it was horrible: that arctic wind knifing in off the ocean, fleas hopping on every living creature in the camp, and the *smells*, ugh—the atmosphere inside those tents was enough to sicken a hog or a goat, smoke and sour milk and wet wool and filthy, unwashed human bodies. You should have warned me beforehand what a winter camp was going to be like. Nothing even resembling a real bath for *months*; Milo, I thought I'd never be able to get the stink off and be clean again!"

Milo took a sip of his cordial. "I don't recall any complaints from you then, Mara."

She laughed throatily. "Of course not, silly. I was in love with you—violently, passionately in love with you. Then, the cold and the stink and the fleas and the filth still added up to paradise . . . just so long as you were there. We women are like that in the first flush of love."

"And now, Mara?" He rolled onto his side to face her. "That was forty years ago. How much do you love me now?"

"Not that much, Milo. That kind of love can never last very long; it's too intense, too demanding, too abrasive on the emotions of both parties. But I do love you still, Milo. Ours has become a . . . a *comfortable* relationship for me. And what of you, my lord?"

Before he answered, he drained the cordial and tossed the silver goblet in the general direction of the table, then rolled onto his back, pillowing his head on his crossed arms, but with his face still toward his wife.

"I didn't love you, Mara, not then, and I think you knew."

She nodded her head slowly, and the fire threw highlights from the blue-black tresses that rippled about her shoulders.

"I knew. But it didn't matter, not then."

"For a long while, Mara, I didn't know if I could ever love you. Not that you were hard to love, that wasn't it. But I feared that my ability to love might have atrophied. I'd been afraid to love any woman for so long, you see.

"It's bad enough with a woman you simply like and respect—watching her, day by day, year by year, grow old and infirm and finally die. When you love that woman, it's the cruelest of tortures. After having suffered that torment a couple of times, Mara, I willed myself not to love.

"But, over the years, I have come to love you, my lady. Not a fiery, passionate love, but a love that has come slowly into being. It is nurtured by my respect for you and my admiration of you, by my faith in your honesty and by the pleasure that your dear companionship has given me. Our relationship is, as you said, a most comfortable one. I *am* comfortable, Mara, and I am very happy. You made me happy, darling, and I love you."

Resting her hand on his cheek, she whispered, "I'm glad you remembered how to love, my Milo, and now that the southern Ehleenoee are all reunited and there will be peace . . ."

'*Hah*!" he exclaimed, sitting up. "Peace, is it, my lady? Such peace as we have now will last until spring, possibly.

Let us hope it's not an early spring, for Greemos and I have much to do."

Mara arched her brows. "Greemos? But he is King Zenos' *Strahteegos*."

"So he is," agreed Milo, "but only until the first day of *Martios*. On that day, I will take his formal oath as the Confederation's new *Strahteegos* of Strahteegoee. Then he and I will ride north and look over the ground on which the army will probably be campaigning."

"But Gabos . . ." she began. "He has served us well, and when he hears . . ."

"Gabos was among the first to know, Mara, and he heartily endorses the move. He'd never admit openly to the fact, of course, but he, of all men, is fully aware that he's getting too old for long campaigns. I'm kicking him upstairs. Week after next, at the Feast of the Sun, I'm investing the old war horse with his new title—*Thoheeks* of the Great Valley.

"That's the only way that we'll ever really secure it, you know. It must be settled and cultivated. I plan one large city and two smaller ones and the majority of their citizens will be, like Gabos, retired soldiers. If they're unmarried, they'll be encouraged to take wives from among the mountain tribes. It worked for the Romans; it should work for me."

"*Romans*?" repeated Mara puzzledly.

"A very warlike people who flourished roughly twenty-four centuries ago, Mara. When they had a difficult frontier to defend, they settled it with old soldiers wed to barbarian girls, which proved quite an effective means of gradually amalgamating their enemies into their empire, as well as providing a certain source of tax revenues rather than expenditures and, at the same time, a virtual breeding ground for the next generation of soldiers."

Suddenly, Mara gurgled with laughter. "Oh, Milo, I just pictured the Lady Ioanna as a country *thoheekeesa*, milking goats instead of coupling with them! Why, she can't even ride; she'll be lost outside a city."

"Which is probably why," announced Milo, "she has been begging Gabos to divorce her, offering him fantastic sums to do so. I advised him to hold out for the highest figure he can get from her, and then to grant her wish. I've already arranged for Gabos to marry Grand Chief Shoomait's youngest daughter. I'm reliably informed that the girl is a nubile four-teen, attractive, intelligent, and personable, and Gabos is not of such an age that he can't beget a few heirs. It's said the girl is the apple of old Shoomait's eye—and God knows she cost the Confederation a high enough bride price. So I think the old bastard will keep his own brigands and the other tribes in check; he's not going to raid his own daughter's lands or try to destroy the inheritance of his grandchildren."

"My, my, husband," teased Mara, "you were certainly a busy little High Lord during those six weeks I spent in the country—creating a new duchy, planning new cities, abetting in the blackmail of an heiress, raiding the Confederation treasury to buy a fourteen-year-old bride for a fifty-year-old man, and arranging to get a new *Strahteegos* just in time for your new war. Tell me, dear heart, who are we fighting this time?"

Frowning, Milo toyed with his signet. "Probably Harzburk, before it's done."

"Harzurk?" she exclaimed. "But the king is your friend, your ally. He sent the second largest body of troops that came from the Middle Kingdoms."

"The King of Harzburk was never my ally, Mara, and I don't think he has ever had a friend," stated Milo. "The only reason he sent me troops was because of his overweening pride and his hereditary enmity toward the Kingdom of Pitzburk, by whom he could not bear to be publicly outdone!

"His goddamned nobles are the reason for it all. They out-numbered the band of Pitzburk nobles and I had to place them at opposite ends of the camp to prevent trouble, even before Zastros' host arrived. Then, when the Southern Council and I had arranged for the withdrawal of their army, those damned fool Middle Kingdoms' fire-eaters rode a little way out of camp and commenced a goddamned pitched battle! If I'd let them, they'd have merrily chopped each other into blood pudding."

"But that's childish," Mara observed. "Why would hundreds of grown men fight for no reason?"

Milo's shoulders rose and fell. "Their kingdoms are hereditary enemies, Mara. I suppose it's in their blood. Why do dogs and cats always fight?"

"Because they're both predators," answered Mara.

"Well, you'll search long and hard to find two more predatory principalities than those two, Mara. I brought their melée to a stop by surrounding them with ten thousand mounted and fully armed dragoons, mostly Freefighters with some Kuhmbuhluhners mixed in, arrowing a few of them to get their attention, then threatening to slaughter every manjack of them if they didn't put up their steel.

"The next morning, I set the Pitzburkers on the march, wounded and all. I sent along Captain Mai and three thousand Freefighter dragoons to 'guide' them and see to it that they switched over to the *western* trade road at Klahkspolis.

"Hardly were they out of camp than those damned Harzburkers had provoked a skirmish with the Eeree nobility. I was out of the *castra* at the time, riding a few miles with Mai and the Pitzburkers, so Greemos and Duke Djefree did the same thing I'd done the day before, except they weren't as careful. They didn't just put arrows into legs and targets and horses—they shot to kill. One of the men they killed was one of King Kahl's many bastards."

Mara groaned. "So now you feel Harzburk will declare war on the Confederation?"

Milo shook his head. "Oh, no, not that sly old buzzard. He's called 'The Fox King' for good reason, though he doesn't quite understand how our Confederation works.

"As you know, Kuhmbuhluhn and Tchaimbuhzburk have boundary disputes that go back decades, but Kuhmbuhluhn's had very little trouble with Getzburk and no one can remember *any* with Yorkburk; yet all three principalities—well-known satellites of Harzburk—have sent heralds to the Duke at Haiguhsburk declaring war, to commence in the spring, as do most Middle Kingdoms' wars.

"Both the Duke and I are convinced that Harzburk is behind these declarations."

Mara tilted her head. "But why doesn't King Kahl just attack Kuhmbuhluhn himself if his people are so fond of fighting?"

"Well, for one thing," said Milo, "because he's not so honest and uncomplicated as you, love. For another, because if he were openly to attack a smaller state, his rival—Pitzburk —would attack him."

"Oh, so Pitzburk is our ally?" she asked, then answered, "Yes, that's right, they were the first to send us troops."

"No," Milo explained patiently. "Pitzburk sent us troops because we're good customers; the Pitzburkers are no more allies than are the Harzburkers."

Frowning with concentration, she finally shook her head sadly. "I'm sorry, Milo, I simply don't understand it all. If Pitzburk isn't our ally, then why would they attack Harzburk if Harzburk were to attack Kuhnbuhluhn?"

Milo drew himself up. "All right, children, tonight's lesson will concern the Middle Kingdoms. These lands are bounded on the south by the river that we call Vohreheeos, on the west by the Sea of Eeree, on the north by the Black Kingdoms and . . ."

"Oh, stop it, Milo!" she burst out. "Stop teasing me and tell me the answer to my question."

He grinned. "I'm trying to, woman, just stop interrupting. Up until the disruptions of the Great Earthquake, three-hundred fifty-odd years ago, the Middle Kingdoms were just that—three big kingdoms: Harzburk in the east; Pitzburk in the west; and Eeree in the north. Subsequent to the disasters of the quake and the subsidence of large chunks of Harzburk and Eeree, these kingdoms fragmented into the beginning of the jumbled patchwork of domains we see today.

"Not having suffered damages equal to those of the other kingdoms, Pitzburk reorganized faster and not only reconquered its breakaway areas, but marched on to subjugate a good half of Harzburk, as well. Frightened by the growing size and strength of Pitzburk, Eeree joined with the unconquered Harzburkers, after about ten years, and the combined armies drove the Pitzburk forces all the way back to their own capital and besieged it there.

"That siege lasted nearly two years and might have finally succeeded, had not several things happened almost simultaneously. Having stripped the surrounding countryside bare, the besiegers ran out of food and began to fight each other, but the Pitzburkers were in such bad shape that they were unable to take advantage of the situation and break the siege. Then an army from the north of the Sea of Eeree laid siege to Eereeburk at the same time that large-scale rebellions erupted in Harzburk; so both armies hurried home.

"The King of Pitzburk had died during the siege and only the common enemy had held the nobles together; with the enemy gone, all hell broke loose in the western kingdom.

"So, what do we have today? There are only two actual kingdoms, Eeree having become a republic; but, though much shrunken in area, Harzburk, Eeree, and Pitzburk are still the major powers in the Middle Kingdoms. Then there are the great duchies. There were sixteen of them before Kuhmbuhluhn joined our Confederation, but all of the remaining ones are in some ways connected to one or the other of the Big Three. Next come the small fries, and some of them are really small, Mara, tiny; but all are more or less independent states and most are ruled by a hereditary nobility—peacock-proud and boasting a veritable catalogue of grandiose titles."

Mara breathed a long, long sigh, saying tiredly, resignedly, "Husband, when are you going to tell me why Pitzburk will attack Harzburk if Harzburk attacks Kuhmbuhluhn?"

Pointedly ignoring this, Milo simply continued. "You and most of the Ehleenoee were horrified that the civil war that racked and wrecked the Southern Kingdom lasted for five years, yet almost the same thing has been going on in the Middle Kingdoms for over three hundred years."

"But that's different, Milo," Mara interjected. "After all, the Southern Kingdom is an Ehleen kingdom, a civilized realm, while the Middle Kingdoms are only an aggregation of brawling barbarians, little higher culturally than the mountain tribes."

"Wrong!" Milo asserted. "Wrong on several counts, Mara. First of all, although the peoples of the Middle Kingdoms and the peoples of the mountain tribes are of the same race, there is a vast cultural gap between them; in fact, it is you Ehleenoee whose culture bears the closest similarity to the mountaineers."

Mara sat up quickly, bristling, her black eyes flashing. "I'll take just so much, Milo, even from you!"

He raised his hand in the gesture of peace. "Hold on, dear, let me explain. What I just said is not completely true, not now, anyway, but it was true as little as thirty-odd years ago. Why do you think I directed the tribe here, rather than to the Middle Kingdoms or the Black Kingdoms or Kehnooryos Mahkehdohnya? Because in warfare, as in too many other aspects, the culture of all the southern Ehleenoee was a static culture, as the culture of the mountain peoples is a static culture."

He, too, sat up. "Mara, many of our people feel that I am unjustly persecuting the Ehleen Church in the Confederation. This is an exaggeration. I'm not persecuting it at all; I'm only trying to weaken the stranglehold it has had on the Ehleenoee and their culture for far too long. An organized religion of any description is, by its very nature, best served by conservatism. This is why, when I gave the ancestors of the Horseclans their laws and religion, I did it in such a manner that it would be very difficult for a priestly caste to develop.

"Your cultural apogee was reached two hundred years ago and you were still squatting there, until the coming of the Horseclans. Your average Ehleen is born a conservative—'What was good enough for great great grandpa is good enough for me!' Between that basic attitude and the tendency of the *Eeyehrefsee* to brand as Satan-spawned any person or thing they don't understand, the creativity has been all but ground out of your people, Mara."

She slapped her thigh angrily. "Now, that is a lie, and you know it! If our people . . . *my* people . . . lack creativity, then from whence comes our art, our music, our literature, our architecture? Why, the very palace in which you sit slandering us is new. Demetrios had most of it built just before you barbarians invaded. Don't misunderstand me, *I* bear little love for Church or *Eeyehrefsee*—the black-robed vultures! Do you know how they 'test' a suspected Undying? They lop off a hand or a foot and plunge the stump into boiling pitch. Then they throw the unfortunate wretch into a dungeon for a couple of months to see if it grows back. No, I wouldn't care if you had every *Eeyehrefs* in the Confederation roasted alive, but I won't have my *people* defamed!"

"Mara," he went on doggedly, "your anger is unworthy of the fine woman I know you are. Stop thinking like an Ehleen and open your mind. Think, Mara, *think*! Your artistics are all nobles, which class is infamously irreligious. No, it is the poor and the oppressed who are your most religious; your peasants, the *khoreekoee*, they are the actual strength of the Church. When did one of them ever come up with something new and different—a labor-saving device, for instance, something great grandpa didn't have?"

He paused, awaiting her answer, but she only sat in sullen silence.

"What would happen if a *khoreekos* devised and fabricated a simple, mule-drawn apparatus that could reap a field of rye in less time than twenty scythe-men? Well, Mara," he prodded, "what would be the fate of that agrarian genius? Would he be lauded for his innovative ability? Would his peers beat a path to his door, that he might show them how to build and use his invention? Answer me, wife!"

"Oh, you know damned well what would happen to the poor dumb bastard, Milo!" snapped Mara. "The *Eeyehrefsee* would see him tortured until he admitted to transactions with Satan . . . or died; then they'd see him and his invention burned together."

"Precisely." He nodded. "Which certainly rather discourages any original thought on the part of the land slaves, doesn't it? But the priests don't intimidate me. I have devised and am going to introduce just such a machine at the next harvest time."

"Oh, Milo, Milo!" Mara pled. "Please don't stir up any more trouble with the Church. You know what they did to that water-powered mill you had built while you were gone last summer. And they'd have seen the millers all slain, too, had my guards not gotten there in time."

"So they sought my millers out in their homes and butchered them before their families," stated Milo grimly. "You didn't know of it because the widows were too terrified to speak until I returned, since the damned *Ehpohteesee* had borne their husbands' mutilated bodies away and promised to come back and do the same to them and their children if they said aught of the murders."

Mara had paled. "*The Knights of the Saints!*" she breathed.

He nodded, tight-lipped. "Yes, the Church's secret terror squads. But the bastards aren't secret any longer; they're all either dead or incarcerated in the old fortress at Goohm."

"But . . ." she stammered, "but how did you find out who they are?"

Milo showed his teeth in a wolf-like grin. "As you said earlier, it's been a busy six weeks for me. I had old Hreesos, the Metropolitan, arrested on a trumped-up charge and immured in the deepest tier of the City Prison, naked, to contemplate upon his sins. After a week, he was brought up, washed, shorn, shaved, and garbed in a death-robe. Then he was left alone for a few minutes, long enough for him to look out the window and see the Chief Executioner sitting on the block and thumbing the edge of his great sword. Mara, you have never heard such moaning and praying," Milo chuckled.

"The old scoundrel went to his knees, wet his red robe down the front, and started going over his life and his more questionable activities in his mind. Of course, he has no mindshield, and I was behind a false wall with two of the prairie cats; Mara, some of the things that swine has done or had done in the name of religion would curl your hair. I'd originally intended fining him and freeing him after I'd picked his mind, but after I found out just what a merciless monster he is, I had him heaved back in his cell. He's far too dangerous to be out of a cage!"

"And I hadn't been back in the palace for an hour when a delegation presented a petition for me to intercede with you on Hreesos' behalf," said Mara. "The delegates who apprised me of the fact that barbarian *kahtahfraktoee* were riding through the streets and sabering every priest they saw—on your order."

"You've never spoken of any of this before tonight, Mara. Why not?" asked Milo.

She matched his predatory grin, tooth for tooth. "I told you, you could roast them all without upsetting me. Besides, I knew you'd tell me all about it in your own time." Her brow wrinkled. "But why that elaborate charade, darling, why didn't you just have him tortured?"

"Torturing a man like that would have accomplished nothing, Mara. The man, for all his misdeeds, is a religious fanatic. He is dead certain that every evil he has wrought has been holy, in that his acts helped perpetuate and strengthen his Church. He would have bitten off his own tongue, ere he imparted to me the information I wanted!"

"So," Mara inquired, "he unknowingly gave you the names of all the *Ehpohteesee*?"

He barked a short laugh. "Hardly! There were over three hundred of the ruffians. But he did think of the Grand Master, his illegitimate son, Marios. Him, I had the pleasure of introducing to the artful Master Fyuhstohn only a couple of hours later. Marios became a real fountain of information. It was all the scribes could do to keep up with him. Then I gave him a cell next door to his father."

"It's all up to you," put in Mara. "But wouldn't it be safer to kill them?"

"That precious pair," snarled her husband, "is undeserving of a quick death. The only man who's allowed to slop those swine is a deaf mute; the guards on the level above have orders to immediately slay anyone, even the prison-governor, who tries to go below—I issued their orders, in person!"

"What," she asked, "are you going to do with the rest of the *Ehpohteesee*?"

"When the Church has been weakened and discredited to the point that witnesses are no longer afraid to come forward, I'm going to try them for their crimes. Until then, I've a number of schemes to keep them busy. Shortly, they'll start repairs on the east trade road. Next spring and summer will come the cleaning and repair of Goohm—at the end of the campaign, I mean Goohm to become Freefighter headquarters. Next winter, they can go back on the roads."

"How in God's name do you propose to finance road work and fortress repairs, Milo?" Mara demanded. "You had to take Lek . . . Lord Alexandros' kind offer of a loan to finish paying off your Freefighters."

"Since your so-called delegation told you so much, they couldn't have failed to mention my 'desecration' of the cathedral." At her nod, he went on. "Inside and under the main altar, we found more than two hundred thousand ounces of gold, mostly in coins, as well as over a million ounces of silver! When we tore apart the Metropolitan's quarters, we found even more gold and enough cut gemstones to cover the top of that table—mostly fine diamonds, with a few rubies and opals and one pouch of very nice emeralds."

Stunned, she could only say, "But . . . but where? How . . . ?"

"Many ways, Mara. Perhaps a twentieth was out of free-will offerings and contributions. As for the rest . . . well, The Holy and Apostolic Church of Kehnooryos Ehlas owns farms, flocks, herds, ships, warehouses, orchards, vineyards, extensive properties in the various cities, at least two quarries . . . and more than half the brothels in the realm! They don't own the brothels openly, of course, but through dummies—willing confederates amongst the laity.

"But there's more. You wouldn't believe the quantities of wine and brandies and cordials we found in Hreesos' cellars, and never a single tax brand on any of them; so, he's obviously been smuggling. But it's his other little side line that really infuriates me."

She had seen that look in his eyes before, but only in battle, and seeing it as they lazed before a fire in their own palace frightened her.

"For most of the twenty years of his primacy, Hreesos and his priests have been offering to take one or two children from large peasant families into the monastic orders; usually, the peasants jumped at the chance, since it promised the children a secure and comparatively easy life, and gave the parents one or two less mouths to feed. From all over the realm, the children so collected would be brought here, the boys to St. Paulos' and the girls to St. Sohfeeah's.

"When they totaled twenty to thirty head, they'd be marched down to the docks and loaded onto one of the Church's ships, which would promptly set sail for *Yee-spahneeah* or *Ghahleeah* or *Yeetahleeah* or even *Pahl'yos Ehlahs*. The prettier ones would be sold to brothels, the others to disreputable types who would either conceal the children's origin or else swear that they were war captives.

"You see, my dear, the Holy Hreesos was also a slaver.

Several of his ship captains have made the acquaintance of
Master Fyuhstohn, subsequent to which they told me a good
deal about their activities. One of them had been at it for
over twelve years, averaging a hundred children each year,
for whom he got high prices, since the priests were careful to
choose only attractive, strong, and healthy children. Those
captains and their crews will also be improving the trade road
and helping the *Ehpohteesee* at Goohm."

"But what about those damned *Eeyehrefsee?*" exploded
Mara. "They *chose* the poor children. Surely they *knew?*"

"Oh, I'm certain that they did know, Mara, but the time is
not yet ripe for me to strike directly at the Church," he replied, adding, "with a war declared for the spring, I don't
need a peasant uprising this winter. No, I'm playing this
business a different way, Mara.

"When I sent Lord Alexandros the principal and interest of
his loan, I sent, as well, a request. Since then, I've dispatched
seven ships to some of the ports mentioned by Hreesos' captains. *My* captains know those ports well; they are shrewd,
hard men and in possession of adequate funds to buy back as
many children as they can locate."

"Oh, yes," she said coldly, "I'm beginning to understand, I
think. You mean to return them home and let them tell their
parents and neighbors all about their 'religious training'? Sun
and Wind, my lord, that's fiendish. Why, those peasants will
tear the *Eeyehrefsee* into gobbets, with no *Ehpohteesee* on
hand to protect them!"

Milo nodded, grinning broadly. "Precisely, my dear. And
don't you think their fierce faith in the Holy and Apostolic
Church and her clergy might be just a wee bit undermined,
eh?"

"Husband-mine, please constantly remind your wife to
never incur the enmity of High Lord Milo of the Confederation." She answered his grin with one of her own.
"Sweetheart, it's a master stroke; the Church won't recover
for decades . . . if ever. But tell me, what was the total value
of Hreesos' hoard?"

"*After,*" he emphasized the word, "I repaid the loan and fi-
nanced the captains, and discounting the smuggled potables

that are now in the palace cellars, the Confederation Treasury shows a balance of some forty million *thrahkmehs*."

"But, Milo!" Mara cried. "He couldn't, simply could not, have amassed so much in only twenty years! *Forty million thrahkmehs, eight* million *tahluhz!*"

"Oh, the current Metropolitan didn't collect it *all*, Mara," Milo assured her. "Sun knows how long his predecessors had been squirreling it away in that altar. Remind me to show you some of those coins that came from bags so old they fell to dust when we touched them. There was one bag of mint-sharp *thrahkmehs* of Lukos The First."

"They must have been saving a long time!" she exclaimed wonderingly. "Why, Lukos has been dead over three hundred years!"

He laughed harshly. "Yes, but Hreesos' successors will never have the opportunity to lay away lucre on that scale. From now on, the Church is going to be taxed, heavily taxed, on all the sundry holdings. We are slowly unraveling the Black Robes' financial empire, and we're nibbling bits and pieces of it away. I've already confiscated the Church's fleet on the basis of evidence of smuggling, and all the harbor warehouses, too. I didn't include the value of those in the treasure balance, but it will up the balance a tad.

"Every *ehkleeseeah*, every monastery, every farm or pasturage or orchard or vineyard or quarry, every rural building or urban property is being cataloged. My agents are going over them with a louse comb, and wherever they uncover evidence of illegal activities, they are empowered to slap the *ehkleeseeahee* and monasteries with a stiff fine, while any of the other categories are to simply be confiscated to the Confederation . . . all except the brothels, that is."

"Why not the brothels?" Mara queried impishly. "Just think, if the Confederation owned the brothels, the High Lord could use them free."

He refused to rise to the jest. "No, I had a better idea. I'm having the Church's ownerships publicized!"

"Oh . . . ohhhh . . . oh, Milo, ohhhhh!" Clutching her sides and roaring with laughter, she rolled back on the cushions. Finally, she sat up, gasping for breath, her eyes streaming. "Oh, Milo, you're really a terrible man, you know? Of course the *Eeyehrefsee* will all deny it, but, people being what they are, no one will believe them." Then she lapsed into another laughing fit.

Arising to his feet, Milo retrieved his goblet and brought the decanter from the table. After refilling for them both, he said, "Laughing Girl, if you can control yourself long enough, I'll tell you why Harzburk will be attacked by Pitzburk if Harzburk attacks Kuhmbuhluhn . . . unless you're no longer interested. . . ."

On a cold, wet, blustery night in mid-March, three men met in a stone-and-timber hunting lodge near the walled city of Haiguhzburk, capital of the Duchy of Kuhmbuhluhn. On the wide, deep hearth, behind a man-high screen of brass wire, the fire was crackling its way into a huge pinelog and the bright light of the blaze illumined the large-scale map spread on the floor before it. Two-score Horseclansmen ringed the old, two-story building, while ten-score of their kindred patrolled the surrounding forest on their tough, shaggy little horses. And farther out, among the dripping trees and soggy underbrush, ranged a dozen of the great prairie cats.

During the months Milo's heterogeneous army awaited Zastros, *Thoheeks* Greemos and Duke Djefree of Kuhmbuhluhn had become fast friends. Now, the new Confederation *Strahteegos* traced the twisting course of the river that bisected the eastern half of the duchy.

"I could wish, Djef, that the army could headquarter at Mahrtuhnzburk and force the enemy to come to us, rather than trying to hold the damned border north of here. You're sure the invasion will come through that area we rode over, are you?"

Duke Djefree was as broad and as muscular as the *Thoheeks*, though nearly two hands shorter and twenty years older. Like most men who often wore both helm and beavor, his cheeks and chin were clean-shaven and his snow-white hair had been clipped within an inch of his scalp. Taking his pipe from between his strong, yellow teeth, he used its mouthpiece as a pointer.

"Oh, yes, Big Brother, if the allies follow the strategy that my spies at all three courts assure me will be followed, this is the only feasible route. They know that they must have all three of their armies combined to defeat mine and the troops they're sure my overlord will loan me."

Greemos' saturnine face mirrored puzzlement. "But how do they know your army will be there to meet them?"

The Duke shrugged his wide shoulders. "Because they know I know they're coming in there; they have as many spies in my court as do I in theirs. That's why we are met here alone tonight with My Lord Milo's men for guards, rather than mine own."

"But, good God, man!" Greemos expostulated explosively. "Think on it! They could be deliberately misleading your agents in the hope that you *will* mass your forces there. Then they could cross the border directly north of either of your principal cities."

Duke Djefree just shook his scarred head calmly. "Oh, no, Brother, they can only attack the old capital from the east. In order to get north of it, they would have to go through Tuhseemark, and Marquis Hwahruhn would never permit their passage, of course."

"He's a friend of yours then, Djef?" probed Greemos. "Does he have enough troops to menace the enemy's flank?"

The Duke rocked back on his heels, laughing. "A friend? Hardly! He'd be overjoyed to hear of my demise, especially were it a slow and painful one." Another laugh bubbled up, and he went on. "As for troops, the last I heard, he boasts all of five hundred pikemen, including his city and frontier guards; he retains a force of all of twenty dragoons, and his family and noble retainers probably number five-and-twenty more. Even were I willing to hire him and his fifth-rate warband, I doubt me they could turn the flank of a muletrain."

"Hell and damnation!" thundered Greemos. "Then what's to prevent Duke Djai from walking right over them and attacking Kuhmbuhluhnburk from the north? A tenth of those three warbands could stamp less than six hundred men into the dust, by God!"

"Because he wouldn't dare attack Tuhseemark, not unless

the Marquis led troops out and attacked him first." Duke Djefree smiled blandly. "Don't you see, Greemos?"

"No, I do not!" snapped the *Thoheeks*. "God's balls, Djef, you make less sense than my wife! Were *I* marching twenty thousand men against you, I'd come any damned way I pleased. I'd send five thousand men and my siege train through Tuhseemark, whether the Marquis liked it or not, and invest Kuhmbuhluhnburk. Then your army would have a grim choice: either meet my main army and take a chance of losing Kuhmbuhluhnburk, and then being taken in the rear by my detached force; or detach part of your smaller army to succor the city, thereby ensuring the defeat of your main force; or withdrawing your entire army toward Kuhmbuhluhnburk, with my army either snapping at your heels or marching on Haiguhsburk."

"Your strategy is good, Big Brother, and I am certain that you would defeat an enemy you so opposed." Duke Djefree spoke slowly, as if to a backward child. "But we may be assured that Duke Djai will not follow such a course. He cannot without the Marquis' leave, and the Marquis will never grant it."

A vein was quivering in Greemos' forehead and his big fists were clenched. But when he would have spoken, Milo laid a hand on his arm.

"Greemos, you Ehleenoee just don't understand these northerners. I'll try to explain and Djef can correct me or bring up any fine points I miss.

"Greemos, within the last seven years you've proved yourself a genius of military strategy and tactics; but, your inborn abilities notwithstanding, you strongly dislike war and your aim is to get it over with as quickly as possible."

"Well, doesn't everyone want peace?" asked the new *Strahteegos*.

Milo shook his head. "No, Greemos, not the Middle Kingdom's nobility. War and fighting have replaced both sport and religion in their lives."

"In fact, Big Brother," interjected the Duke, "war has become religion. The Cult of the Sword has displaced all of the older beliefs, save only worship of The Blue Lady, but she's only worshipped by women, anyway."

"Just so," agreed Milo. "And, like any religion, it has innumerable rules and customs and usages, many of which appear idiotic to the uninitiated. But, Greemos, if you stand back and look deeper than the façade of mere custom, you'll see that there are very good reasons for these rules and usages."

"Your pardon, my lord," said Greemos, "but *what* am I to look into?"

"Bear with me, Lord *Strahteegos*, bear with me," Milo smilingly enjoined him. "Toward the end of their existence, the original three Middle Kingdoms were ruled by tyrannic despots, hated and feared by people and nobility alike. When the Great Earthquake and the chaos it and the floods engendered gave the lords and cities an opportunity for independence, they grasped it, lost it back briefly, then secured it for good and all. They . . ."

Milo paused, then turned to the Duke. "Djef, you're an initiate of the Cult. Perhaps you can explain it somewhat better than can I. What I know is but heresay."

The Duke nodded brusquely. "As you wish, my lord. Look you, Greemos, what it boils down to is this: a smaller state may attack a larger, but a larger state may not attack a smaller except in retaliation for overt attack. D'you ken? A smaller state may enter into compact with one or more others of comparable size to attack a larger, which is just what is being done to me, but if they lose, then all of them are open to attack by the state they attacked. But should a larger state attack a smaller, unprovoked—and such hasn't happened in Sword knows when—things will get rather sticky for him in rather short order. It may start even before he attacks, for when his intent is obvious all Sword Initiates are bound by Sword oath to desert him, which means most if not all of his Freefighters. If this fails to deter him, if his force contains enough non-initiates and oath-breakers for him to actually launch an attack against the smaller state, then he is certainly dead and his dynasty as well, probably. All surrounding states, large and small, will march against him and his lands and titles will be forfeited to the ruler he attacked. If he fails to die in battle, then he will be hauled before a tribunal of the Cult, who will decide the manner of his execution. Likewise, all other oath-breakers in his service. Non-initiates are not subject to Cult discipline.

"So, you see, Big Brother, Kuhmbuhluhnburk is quite safe, unless our army should be defeated, for Duke Djai is an Initiate and no fool."

15

Duke Djai and his allies, Counts Hwahltuh of Getzburk and Mortuhn of Yorkburk, unsuspectingly marched their twenty-two thousand men directly into the jaws of *Strahteegos* Greemos' carefully prepared trap. The security measures had been stringent—a thing almost unheard of in Middle Kingdoms' wars—the inevitable spies and double agents having been spoon-fed information to the effect that the Confederation had sent Kuhmbuhluhn about five thousand troops, mostly Ehleen infantry, a tenth of the Confederation's standing army. Since this was the percentage usually loaned to a vassal state by an overlord, Duke Djai swallowed the tale.

The bait—the Army of Kuhmbuhluhn and its apparent reinforcements—stood athwart the valley through which Duke Djai must advance, their shallow formations lapping up the slopes of the flanking hills.

Duke Daji—tall, slender, and wiry, his full armor painted a brilliant blue and gilt-edged—sat his horse beneath the rippling folds of his silken banner, observing the waiting foe, while his own host reformed from marching to battle order. Ranged to his right and left were his allies—Count Hwahltuh, in violet and silver, and Count Mortuhn in orange and black.

Count Hwahltuh had just respectfully opined that Duke Djefree was too expert a war leader to place his men so stupidly—not deep enough to stop cavalry, nor yet long enough in the line to prevent flanking.

Duke Djai threw back his head and his high, tenor laughter pealed. Grinning under his sweeping, red-blond mustache, he answered, "Hwahlt, you're getting old and suspicious. What else could our esteemed cousin of Kuhmbuhluhn do? If he'd massed his slender forces in one of the narrower valleys, we'd have come through this one and taken him in the rear. His expertise told him that, so he did what he could with what he had. We'll triumph, of course, but his new Ehleen overlord should have sent him more men."

Milo, Lord Alexandros of the Sea Isles, and the Sea Lord's lieutenant, Yahnekos, sat in an artfully concealed vantage point at the crest of the hill on the bait's right flank, from whence they witnessed the entirety of the blood-drenched affair.

Duke Djai waited nearly an hour for the flankscouts to report, but when they had not returned by the time the army was formed, he recklessly began his advance. After all, how could Duke Djefree have laid a trap when *all* of his force was arrayed in plain sight at the other end of the valley?

To the watchers, that advance was a colorful and stirring spectacle—the noblemen in the lead, their painted or enameled armor and nodding plumes and snapping banners creating a rainbow-hued kaleidoscope; behind the banners rode the personal entourages, then rank on rank of Freefighter dragoons and lancers; at a lengthening distance trotted disciplined units of light and heavy infantry.

"Have they no archers?" asked Alexandros. "Or slingers or engines to soften up the opposition?"

Smiling grimly, Milo shook his head. "No, they consider weapons that can kill at a distance to be dishonorable and only use them in defenses and sieges. They have both longbow men and crossbow men, but they probably left them to defend their train."

At a distance of five hundred yards from the waiting Kuhmbuhluhn array, Duke Djai halted to dress ranks for the final charge as well as to permit his infantry to catch up; for while a cavalry charge could break the formation of an opposing army, he knew full well that only infantry could complete the rout and consolidate the victory.

Count Hwahltuh sidled his black charger up to Duke Djai's

gray stallion. "By your leave, my lord, their lines appear to have deepened in the center. I have a foreboding feeling about this assault."

Duke Djai was in high good humor and not even the doubt and worry tinging the young count's voice could dampen it. Slapping gauntleted hand upon armored thigh, he laughed. "You're too gloomy, little cousin. Of course, Duke Djefree has deepened his center, but you can bet he's stripped any depth from his flanks to do it! The foot already have their orders, as do the lancers. When we strike the center, they'll advance on the flanks. I'll have reconquered Haiguhzburk within the month, our dear Lord will be revenged, and both you and Mortuhn will be considerably richer. Now, get your people straightened out and stop fretting so."

For the first hundred yards they moved at a brisk walk, in time to a sprightly tune shrilled by the flutes and fifes of the musicians who followed the infantry. When the horsemen commenced to slow trot, the fifers cased their instruments, unslung their shields, and drew their swords, while the drummers remained halted in formation, beating time for the foot.

A few arrows from the defending force were to be expected, so Duke Djai was not alarmed when a drizzle of shafts pelted down, but that drizzle rapidly increased to a shower and, suddenly, the sky was dark with feathered death. Duke Djefree could not possibly have so many archers! But he knew what must be done and turning in his saddle, bade the sounding of the charge, for the only certain way to escape an arrow storm was to close with the enemy so that the cowardly bowmen could not loose for fear of downing their own troops.

The horn pealed its command and the steel-edged formation swept forward at the gallop, the bass rumble of tens of thousands of hooves clearly audible to the High Lord and the Sea Lord in their eyrie high above. The lines wavered but little, rough ground notwithstanding, as the riders of faster horses held them back to match the pace of slower mounts. Their shouts and war cries were almost lost in the overall din, as the forms of all but the first ranks were, in the rolling clouds of dust.

The living *tsunami* crashed against the dense hedge of

pikemen with a noise loud even to the watchers on the hill-tops—sounds of metal hard-swung on metal, screams of man and screams of horse. The lines of the defenders bowed in-ward . . . inward . . . inward, then snapped back with the weight of reinforcements, while the right and left wings ran down the hillsides to flank the milling, hacking horsemen.

Up the valley to the north, what was left of twelve thou-sand infantry were formed into a shield-overlapped hedgehog, their pikes and spears fending off squadrons of Confederation *Kahtahfraktoee* and Horseclansmen. The surviving lancers—all Freefighters and recognizing the stench of defeat—stampeded out of the valley, arriving at the train with shouted warnings of the disasters taking place behind them.

Those wagoneers who valued their lives slashed apart the harnesses of the draft mules, then had to fight for possession of them with hordes of archers and crossbow men, as did more than a few lancers have to battle to retain their lathered horses. This internecine warfare was still going on when the main body of the Confederation cavalry, under Sub-*Strahtee-gos* Portos, plowed into them.

When the High Lord and his entourage rode onto the bat-tlefield, it was to find most of the noblemen of three states dead or dying. Ahead of them, to the right of the center, ringed about by hostile swords and pikes, waved the slashed and ragged battle flags of Tchaimbuhsburk and Getzburk. Beneath them, perhaps a score of nobles and a few hundred retainers and dragoons stood afoot or sat drooping mounts—horses and men alike, hacked, bloody, exhausted, but deter-mined to die honorably.

At the High Lord's word, a Kuhmbuhluhn herald rode to within a few yards of the battered survivors of the cavalry charge. Drawing rein, he requested Swordtruce and an-nounced that his lord wished words with Duke Djai.

He was informed that, as Duke Djai had died a few minutes before, it would be most difficult for Duke Djefree to converse with him; however, if the Duke would settle for speech with a mere count, he could be obliged. In any event, the speaker added, a Swordtruce would be more than wel-come, so far as he was concerned.

Two hours later, the speaker, still in his dust-dimmed,

dented, and gore-splattered violet armor, sat in a camp chair across a table from the High Lord of the Ehleen Confederation. Between them, their two sheathed swords lay crossed, significant of a Swordtruce.

"I await your answer, Count Hwahltuh," Milo gently prodded. "Or do you wish leave to think over my offer and to discuss it with your comrades?"

The younger count opened his mouth to speak, but his dry throat produced but a croak, then a spasm of coughing.

Duke Djefree, at Milo's left, shoved a silver ewer of watered wine forward, saying mock-reprovingly, "Oh, cousin, stop being a proper gentleman and drain off a couple of cups of this; your gullet will appreciate it."

Thus given leave, the count quaffed two full pints and part of a third, then said in an unbelieving voice, "You really mean it, my lord? It's not some cruel jest or another trap?"

"Yes, Count Hwahltuh, I do mean it. If you and the other noblemen will take Swordoath to never again bear arms against the Ehleen Confederation, all are free to depart this duchy. You may retain your arms and as much personal baggage as one packmule can bear. If your mount be slain or crippled, I will provide you another for the journey."

The red-haired boy—he couldn't be older than eighteen, reckoned Milo—shook his head in happy wonderment. "You are most generous, my lord. I am certain that Earl Ahrthuh and all the rest would second me in that statement, but what of our people—our retainers and the Freefighters?"

Milo smiled. "They're as free as are you, unless they decide to enlist under the Confederation banner. As for generosity, it is both easy and pleasant to be generous with men who have fought as valiantly as did you and yours."

The young nobleman's face flushed nearly the color of his hair. "Those were kind and most gentle words, Lord Milo. When and where are our ransoms to be paid . . . and have you decided upon the various amounts of them?"

"I demand no ransoms," said Milo flatly. "Nor will my army set one foot on the soil of either Getzburk or Yorkburk, so long as you and they remain true to your oaths. I will march into Tchaimbuhzburk only if King Kahl takes it into his head to march; if he does, the war will be fought on the lands of *his* vassals; there'll be no more fighting in Kuhmbuh-luhn or any other state of the Confederation."

"But . . . but Tchaimbuhzburk and Yorkburk and my own holdings, or an agreed-upon amount of gold, are yours—or, at least, Duke Djefree's—by Swordright!" argued Count Hwahltuh. "And . . ."

"And, were it up to me," Duke Djefree leaned toward the count, smiling, "I'd take all three of them, the lands, not the money; with two duchies and two counties, I could style my-self 'Arch-Duke,' and spit in the Fox King's bloodshot eye with impunity.

"But, Cousin Hwahltuh, Lord Milo is my overlord, I am Sword-oathed to his service, and he wants no more lands north of the Southern River."

"Forgive me, my lord," Count Hwahltuh said, addressing Milo, "but I don't understand really. My Getzburk is a rich county, richer than Yorkburk, by far. The Duchy of Tchaim-buhzburk is . . ."

"Pardon my interruption, please, young man," said Milo in friendly tones. "But if I took, or allowed Duke Djefree to take, the two counties and the duchy, I could depend on a war to retain them every other year for the next fifty, at least. I now rule an area far larger than all of the lands of the Middle Kingdoms combined. Consequently, I've more than enough to occupy my mind without getting involved in you northerners' affairs."

"Yet, when we threatened Duke Djefree," commented Count Hwahltuh thoughtfully, "you did not simply loan him troops; you personally led your entire army to his defense."

Milo nodded. "So I did, young sir, and for a very good reason. I wish to, hereby, serve notice that my Confederation will not tolerate attacks on any of its member-states by any non-member, large or small. I think that that slaughter in the valley was necessary to make my point clear."

"Yes, my lord." Count Hwahltuh speedily agreed. "You as-suredly made clear your intentions to resist aggression against your vassals." Slowly, he poured his cup full again, took a few sips, then suddenly asked, "My Lord Milo, I can see your reason for not wishing to be saddled with *conquered* lands, but . . . but what if . . . if a landholder wished to Swordoath his allegiance to your Confederation, as has Duke Djefree? Would you accept his fealty?"

Milo did not need to enter the boy's mind to define his meaning. In his own mind, he spread out the map of this part of the Middle Kingdoms as they were today. He had taken Kuhmbuhluhn into the Confederation in order to protect his northwest from forays backed by the King of Pitzburk, who had threatened Kehnooryos Ehlahs up until eleven years ago when old King Ehvrit had died and been replaced by the current and friendlier monarch.

Now the threat was Harzburk, and the long, narrow duchy of Kuhmbuhluhn covered less than half of the stretch through which King Kahl might march. The addition of Getzburk, which adjoined Kuhmbuhluhn on north and east, would leave only the county of Yorkburk—a good proportion of which was saltmarsh or freshwater fens—to provide an uncontested access to Kehnooryos Ehlahs.

"Let us be blunt, young sir," he answered. "Do you wish to become my vassal? Would you have your county a member of the Confederation? If you are now willing to renounce your oaths to King Kahl, how can I be assured that you will not forswear those given me when it suits you?"

In a quick flash of the hot temper for which his race was noted, Count Hwahltuh crushed the pint cup in his powerful right hand, unaware of his action until the remaining wine gushed over his skin. "Please accept my apology, my lord. I will replace the cup. But no man of my house has ever been truly named 'forsworn'! *My* oaths were to Duke Djai, who lies dead in yonder valley; *his* oaths were to King Kahl. While the Duke lived, King Kahl had no reason to take my oaths himself.

"And, yes, my lord, I would be your vassal, and you would have me and mine."

So, in the forty-first year of his reign, did Milo Morai, High Lord of the Confederation, secure his northern border; for the nephew of the deceased Count of Yorkburk, upon being apprised of Getzburk's new allegiance, was quick to point out that, were *he* Count of Yorkburk—and he had as good a claim as any living man—he would be overjoyed to swear himself and his county to the Confederation. Thus, Milo took young, Earl Ahrthuh's oath, confirmed him Count of Yorkburk, and loaned him Sub-*Strahteegos* Portos and four squadrons of *kahtahfraktoee* to overawe any opposing relatives.

As the High Lord's dromonds clove the waves toward the former Southern Kingdom, he had good cause to be well pleased. Within two years he had avoided the bulk of two invasions and quadrupled the size of the Confederation by the additions of most of his former foes. He had only to add the Sea Isles and the Confederation would include all the southern Ehleenoee.

He smiled then, recalling his last conversation with Mara. Between her and Aldora, Alexandros and his Council of Captains would certainly be pledging their swords—and, more importantly, their ships and nautical expertise—to the Confederation before winter roughened the sea lanes.

His only source of discomfiture lay deep in the forbidding reaches of that vast wasteland of saltswamps that held the J. & R. Kennedy Center. Despite his warning to the Senior Director, he was dead certain that he'd not seen the last of them. But any attempt to take either an army or a fleet against their unknown powers would probably be suicidal. So he could only await their next move, hoping that he would know it for what it was when it came.